THE
COWBOY'S
Belated Discovery
SADDLE SPRINGS ROMANCE - BOOK 5

VALERIE COMER

Greenwords Media

Valerie Comer Bibliography

Urban Farm Fresh Romance

0. Promise of Peppermint (ebook only)
1. Secrets of Sunbeams
2. Butterflies on Breezes
3. Memories of Mist
4. Wishes on Wildflowers
5. Flavors of Forever
6. Raindrops on Radishes
7. Dancing at Daybreak
8. Glimpses of Gossamer

Christmas in Montana Romance

1. More Than a Tiara
2. Other Than a Halo
3. Better Than a Crown

Farm Fresh Romance

1. Raspberries and Vinegar
2. Wild Mint Tea
3. Sweetened with Honey
4. Dandelions for Dinner
5. Plum Upside Down
6. Berry on Top

Saddle Springs Romance
(Montana Ranches Christian Romance)

1. The Cowboy's Christmas Reunion
2. The Cowboy's Mixed-Up Matchmaker
3. The Cowboy's Romantic Dreamer
4. The Cowboy's Convenient Marriage
5. The Cowboy's Belated Discovery
6. The Cowboy's Reluctant Bride

Garden Grown Romance
(Arcadia Valley Romance)

1. Sown in Love (ebook only)
2. Sprouts of Love
3. Rooted in Love
4. Harvest of Love

Riverbend Romance Novellas

1. Secretly Yours
2. Pinky Promise
3. Sweet Serenade
4. Team Bride
5. Merry Kisses

valeriecomer.com/books

CHAPTER 1

W hy were there always weddings?
Weddings, where hopes and dreams and starry gazes gouged Garret Morrison's soul, shattered by memories of screeching, tearing metal and a scream cut short. Weddings, the hurricane-force winds that slammed against every boulder he'd added to the stone wall of protection. Not just his protection, no. The protection of anyone he might dare to love.

Garret forced his hands to roam the grand piano's keyboard while he gathered control and awaited further instruction. Evening sunlight angled low through the church's circular stained glass window, casting a multi-hued glow over the sanctuary, empty except for the two women in jeans and T-shirts.

"You're thinking *Ode to Joy* as a wedding processional? Hmm." Tori Carmichael tapped her jaw as she squinted at the knotty pine ceiling.

"Trevor and I love that song." The bride-to-be cast a

beseeching glance at Garret. "It means so much to both of us."

He pretended not to notice. They'd come to a decision then he'd do what he was told. Long years of experience had made him good at keeping a neutral expression.

Unlike Tori Carmichael. Everything that woman thought was displayed across her face in living technicolor, but she was also willing to describe it in excruciating detail. Any day now she'd get tired of silently mooning over Garret and either confess her adoration to him, or turn her attention to a more likely candidate.

Please, oh, please choose Option #2. Not that she wasn't sweet and pretty. She definitely was, but she didn't deserve the likes of him.

"It could work for the bridesmaids." Tori nodded firmly and turned to Denae Archibald. "But since you've always said you wanted a very traditional ceremony, I still think you should come down the aisle to *Here Comes the Bride* yourself."

Garret's fingers took their cue from her words, morphing the random notes into the time-honored wedding march. A single guy of thirty shouldn't know this piece of music as well as he did. At how many of his friends' weddings had he played now? Too many. Not that he resented their happiness.

It just wasn't for him. He'd had his chance.

He tuned out the two women who stood just below the platform in deep conversation. The wedding was still two weeks off, and the final decision didn't matter to him. At first Denae had wanted a string quartet to come in from Missoula. Her fiancé had convinced her to save the strings for the dance and let Garret do the honors for the ceremony.

The honors? If only they knew.

He forced his attention to the piano and played the march through a second time then slid back into *Ode to Joy*.

No one had questioned the reasons a young man might uproot his previous life and move to a western Montana community with his retired parents. Many guys around Saddle Springs worked on the ranches where they'd grown up, preparing to take over one day. His new friends thought he was easy-going. Maybe that he had no ambition, or even no past. Their impressions didn't matter. He knew the truth, but if he kept busy enough, kept his defenses strong enough, he could avoid dwelling on it.

Weddings were the hardest things.

"What do you think?" Denae's voice came from close beside Garret's shoulder.

Only decades of practice kept his hands steady on the keyboard at the collision of two worlds. He turned to Denae. "About what?"

"Tori's idea."

He'd blanked their voices. Now he scrambled to catch up. His fingers seemed to have heard, though. They sought and found a transition between the two melodies. "Like this?"

Denae stared at Garret's hands then back at his face. "How do you do that? I didn't hear you practicing. You must have linked those pieces before."

Garret stilled. How could he explain when he himself

had no idea? He offered a little shrug. "Is that the concept you're looking for? Because I can try something else if you prefer." He launched back into the closing measures of *Ode to Joy* and found a different segue into the wedding march, raising his eyebrows at the bride as he played.

Beside Denae, Tori swept long brown hair over her shoulder. "You're good, Garret. I like that."

Liked that he was good? Liked the arrangement he was creating on the fly? No need to wonder. With her, it was both. Everything. Always.

The groom's youngest brother would soon be home for Trevor and Denae's wedding. Sawyer was close to Tori's age. They'd both grown up here in Saddle Springs' ranching country, unlike Garret. They were even paired together for the wedding. Maybe they'd spark a renewed friendship when romance already danced in the air. That would be good, right? Then people could stop speculating about her and Garret, which had seemed inevitable since they were the only two singles left in their group.

Maybe he needed new buddies to hang out with. Ones already married.

"Play through it again, Garret?" asked Denae. "Tori and I will take turns coming down the aisle to get an idea how many times you need to play it before switching to the wedding march."

"You and I are going to be all three bridesmaids and the bride?" Tori's eyebrows peaked.

"Sure, why not? But I get to be the bride." Winking, Denae gave Tori a side-hug. "Thanks for helping me with this. I owe you big time."

Tori squeezed her back, her gaze flicking to Garret's.

Her eyes were hazel, somewhere between brown and green and gold. He filed that info away then mentally trashed the observation, scoffing lightly. Why bother to remember? It didn't matter.

She narrowed her gaze at his muffled snort.

He stared just past her head as though the distant back pew was the most fascinating object in the world.

It needed to be.

TORI PRETENDED to be the maid of honor, proceeding down the church aisle for the second time, fake-carrying an imaginary bouquet against her comfy T-shirt. Denae, who'd just marched as bridesmaid number two, dashed past her to the back of the sanctuary and waited for the music to transition to the wedding march. Tori found the masking-tape x on the platform's low carpet and turned to face the bride.

Music poured from the piano, the sound so complex, so full, it seemed four hands played instead of two. She didn't need to see Garret's face to imagine his focus as his fingers flew over the keyboard. She'd memorized every angle of his jaw ages ago. He didn't seem to know she existed, even though they'd chatted one-on-one plenty of times over the past several years.

Was she some kind of idiot? Who hung around for years waiting for a guy to notice her? A stupid woman, that's who. And Tori wasn't stupid. She needed a game plan, and then she needed to step out on a limb and execute it. Either that or forget about Garret Morrison.

This impromptu practice was faker than even a wedding rehearsal, but Denae could hardly have fit a wider grin on her face as she strolled toward Tori if it were the real thing. She was absolutely head over heels for Trevor Delgado, and it showed even when he wasn't in the building. Denae had spent the entire year of their engagement meticulously planning her ideal day to the tiniest detail.

Tori didn't need that much perfection. She'd rather elope like Carmen and Spencer had done last fall, but her parents would never forgive her. At this rate, they were going to die of old age waiting for someone to take their baby girl off their hands, but they were nowhere near the age of Garret's folks.

The music drifted away, and Denae pumped her fist as she pivoted toward the piano. "That was perfect! Thanks, Garret. I knew you'd nail it."

"Yeah, I think it worked fine."

His baritone voice was so dusky, Tori shivered. Certainly not from chill on a warm spring evening.

"So I'm playing for James and Lauren's duet..." Papers shuffled. "I've run through that with them a few times."

Finally an excuse to look at him. "They sound really good together."

Garret nodded but didn't glance her way. "And then I've got *The Love of God* for the candlelighting ceremony. Right?"

"Yes." Denae slid onto the bench beside him. "Two or three minutes, maybe? It won't take long."

He jotted a note.

"That leaves just the recessional for you." Denae nudged Garret. "You're off duty for the reception, so you can just kick back and enjoy it. Ask a pretty girl to dance." She winked at Tori.

"I'm not much for dancing." His face blanked. "Two left feet."

"Oh, I doubt that." Tori perched on the edge of the platform. "I'm sure you've got the moves."

"You'd lose that bet."

Tori was failing already, since he wouldn't even look at her. But she'd get him out onto that dance floor if she had to trip and fall in his arms to force him there. It was her new calling in life. Mission: make-Garret-look-at-her.

"Anything else?" asked Denae.

Garret shook his head and glanced at his watch. "We're good. James will be here in a few minutes to practice for Sunday morning worship."

"Okay. We'll get out of your hair." Denae linked her arm with Tori's and dragged her to the entry where they'd left their purses on a table.

"See you!" Tori hollered toward Garret, but he'd already immersed back into music and didn't look up.

"That guy," muttered Denae as they left the building. "He's really something, but his social skills? Not so much."

"Tell me."

Denae narrowed her gaze at Tori. "And yet..."

Oops. "And yet what?"

"Has he ever asked you out?"

Tori shook her head, maybe a little too hard. "I'm pretty sure he doesn't know I exist."

Denae grinned. "And you wish he'd notice?"

Tori hip-checked her friend. "Stop it."

"I can't help myself. I edit romance novels for a living, remember? I see hearts and ribbons and fluttering eyelashes everywhere."

"I don't think it's meant to be." But that was a heart-breaking thought. He was such a great guy. He helped out with the Cowboy Santa program every year, and anytime someone needed a hand. And the way he took care of his aging parents? Wow. He had such a soft heart toward anyone in need. Maybe he didn't figure Tori needed anything, but she did. The love of a kind heart like his.

"Hmm. Let me have a look at you." Denae stopped in the middle of the church parking lot, put her hands on her slim hips, and gave Tori a slow once-over.

"Umm... hello. I'm still here."

"Have you tried short hair?" Denae fingered Tori's long strands. "I can see you with a sassy cut, maybe with a tint of red to liven it up. And some new clothes. You've got a great figure. We can show that off a little."

"Right. Have you forgotten I earn my keep taking kids on trail rides and mucking out stalls? There's a reason for the jeans and T-shirts."

Denae rolled her eyes. "Not twenty-four-seven, I hope. I mean, you're here now, not riding."

"A favor to a friend." Tori grinned at the bride-to-be. "I guess you're right, though. Living on the ranch makes me a little lazy." She finger-combed her hair back from her temples. "You really think I could pull off short?"

"Yes! Lauren's mom is a whiz at cute cuts. Plus, she'll keep you entertained the whole time you're in Shear

Inspirations. I'm zipping into Missoula on Monday. Any chance you can get the day off and come with me? I would love to take you shopping."

"Aren't you too busy running wedding errands? You're down to two weeks."

"Never too busy for a friend. It would be nice to think about something else for a few hours."

Tori examined Denae's face. Nothing showed to make her think her friend didn't mean it. "You know what? I'll see if Mom and Dad can spare me for the day. The guest cabins aren't full yet — not like they will be in a week or two when schools everywhere are done for the year."

"Let's do it!" Denae hiked her eyebrows and pointed her thumb toward the church. "Garret Morrison isn't going to know what hit him."

Maybe it was a chance to get his attention, just once. How could she resist?

CHAPTER 2

G arret shoved his hat back on his head and rested his booted foot on the lowest rail of the white board fence surrounding the pasture. Four horses, including his favorite mare, Trudy, pranced around like they'd never seen green grass before. They hadn't... at least not since yesterday.

Not that he had time to watch the horses at play. He needed to clean out the stalls and rotate the next group and then the next. Several of the mounts needed solid exercise today. What was it with owners who rarely showed up? Just because they boarded their horses at Canyon Crossing Stables didn't mean they should abdicate all responsibility, but many of them did, adding to Garret's workload.

With his father's declining health, more and more fell on Garret's shoulders. He needed to talk to Dad about hiring help at least part-time.

A black pickup emblazoned with a farrier's logo turned into the drive. Garret shook his head. He must

have misplaced a week somewhere. So much for uninter-
rupted cleaning time... but maybe work would run late
enough he'd have an excuse not to go to dinner with his
friends. He used to enjoy it, until Tori began paying attention to him a few months back. She was getting harder
and harder to avoid and ignore.

Garret dredged up a smile and strode over to the
farrier's truck just as the lean cowboy emerged from the
driver's side.

"Noah Cavanagh!" Garret held out his hand. "You
pulled it off. Good for you."

With a broad grin, the younger man returned his grip.
"Yes, sir. Finished my training and put old Rusty out to
pasture. I have to say I'm mighty grateful to him for
taking a greenhorn under his wing and giving me the
chance to prove myself."

"I've seen your work under Rusty's watchful eye, and
I'm confident you're well able to handle our horses on
your own. Between ours and those on board, we've got
fourteen at the moment."

Noah nodded. "I doubt I can get them all in one day,
but I've got a room booked at the Hats Off Motel and
some horses to tend at the Flying Horseshoe this week as
well. I'll be in Saddle Springs a few days."

"And you'll be through every six weeks like Rusty
was?"

"About that, if it's all right with you?"

"Sure thing." Garret waved to a cement pad next to
the corral. "If you want to park in the shade there, you
can get started anytime. I'll give my dad a holler, and he
can give you a hand with the horses. I've got a full roster

myself today." Thankfully Dad had slept better last night and might be up for the work. He'd enjoy talking young Cavanagh's ear off at the very least.

"I'll get set up then." Noah gave a nod and hopped back in his truck.

Garret jogged up the steps and into the house he'd vacated not half an hour before. "Dad? Can you give the farrier a hand? It's Noah Cavanagh. Remember him? He worked with Rusty the past year or two."

"Who?" His father's tired-sounding voice came through the archway.

Garret hurried into the living room as his father struggled to get the recliner upright. "You okay?"

Dad blinked. "I think so. You caught me dozing."

"Sorry. We can manage without you." He really couldn't. Not assist Noah and clean the stables and exercise the horses.

"I'm coming." Dad shuffled over to the fridge and helped himself to a bag of cut apples.

"I just put a few out in the pasture. You can run them through first."

Dad nodded and made his way out the door and down the steps.

Garret watched him amble toward the fence, where Noah was lifting the side of the truck box to expose his portable blacksmith shop. The two of them would be fine, and he could get back to the stables.

If his music school prof could see his hands now, clad in leather gloves, shoveling manure and tossing hay bales, she'd turn over in her grave. Had he made the right decision when his world in Kentucky had upended? It had happened around the time that his dad — or, at least, the only dad he'd ever known — had become restless in his well-deserved retirement. Or so he'd said.

The riding stable in a small western town had seemed like a place Garret could lick his wounds in peace, but he'd never intended to stay. He'd return to the limelight when his parents were settled into their new routines, but Mom had a brush with cancer then pneumonia had nearly claimed Dad and, before he knew it, Garret seemed to have made Saddle Springs his permanent residence.

It wasn't a bad life. He'd gotten involved in music ministry in the church and made some good friends through it. Friends who were getting hitched left, right, and center. Next week Trevor, the last of his single buddies, would tie the knot.

Just the thought gave Garret an itch. Not to find a woman of his own again — anything but that, no matter how tempting Tori Carmichael's smile — but to head far from Montana and pour everything into recapturing the promising career he'd left behind. Alone.

It was too late for a second chance with the band in Nashville, thanks to Chantelle Devereaux. It was too late for everything, really. Whatever Garret prized had been torn from his grasp one way or another. Best just to hold back and not get invested ever again. For his own protection. For the protection of those around him.

The only ones he couldn't shield were Tuck and Nancy Morrison, but he could give his parents as much security and love and peace of mind as they'd given him as a small traumatized child. He owed them his life, and the debt would not be paid in full until they both drew their final breaths in the most comfort possible.

He'd fail at that, too, of course, but he'd try. As God was his witness, he'd do his best.

Dad ducked between the fence rails and whistled. Trudy trotted over, her head high, her mane fluttering in the breeze. She was a beauty, nuzzling Dad and accepting a slice of apple. The old man hadn't lost his touch yet. He led the mare toward the gate, snagging a halter from a fence post on the way by.

Noah and Dad could handle the shoeing.

Garret stuck in his earbuds, found his favorite worship playlist, and cranked the volume high on his way into the stable. He pushed the wheelbarrow in front of Trudy's box stall and grabbed the wide broom.

This was the world he'd chosen five years back. It was a good place, a solitary spot on God's green earth where a guy could mend his broken heart, his broken spirit, his broken life. Or learn to live with them.

TORI PARKED her RAV4 in front of The Branding Iron Bar and Grill. A quick glance around showed no signs of Garret's red pickup.

Did she *want* to see Garret? She'd bought this outfit with him in mind, but she'd had plenty of time for second thoughts. Third thoughts, really. She glanced down at her legs, only half-covered by the quite short jean skirt Denae had talked her into buying on Monday, right after dumping two-thirds of her previous wardrobe into the receiving bin at a thrift store. There'd been no going back.

She slid out of the vehicle, grabbed her purse, and locked up before tugging the hem a little. The skirt wasn't *that* short. It was longer than most of her shorts, and those were more than decent.

Her brother and sister-in-law's orange Wrangler peeled into the parking lot and whisked into the spot next to Tori. Lauren's eyes widened, and she jumped out of the passenger side before James could come around for her door. Before he'd even shut off the engine, actually.

Lauren parked her hands on her hips and whistled. "Look at *you*! So that's what you and Denae were up to in the big city. That girl loves to shop, and she sucked you right into her vortex." She spun her finger. "Let me see."

Obediently, Tori pivoted, a flush on her cheeks that even a layer of her new makeup likely couldn't hide. "You like?"

When she came around again, her brother stood at the back of the Wrangler studying her with his arms crossed.

"It's so cute." Lauren flicked at James's cowboy hat. "Doesn't your sister look amazing?"

His eyebrows tilted up. "Have Mom and Dad seen you yet?"

Whatever that was supposed to mean. "Mom saw the haircut but not every outfit we bought." Not this one.

"I'm sure your mom will love everything." Lauren nudged her husband. "I adore the reddish tinge in your hair. My mom hinted she'd given you a makeover, but wouldn't spill the details. And that mango top is totally your color. Looks great with your jean jacket. I wonder if I could pull something like that off." Lauren flashed a grin at James then thumbed toward the restaurant door. "Well, let's go in. I see Trevor's truck, and I have questions for Denae."

James gestured for Tori to go first, so she grabbed courage out of thin air and strode across the parking lot. Her brother reached past her to get the door for her and Lauren then Tori paused a moment, allowing her eyes to adjust to the dimmer lighting inside.

Denae waved from their favorite long table in the middle of the busy space, a booth with access from both ends. Beside her sat Trevor and his youngest brother, Sawyer.

Tori blinked. Sawyer? What was he doing in Saddle Springs a week before the wedding? In the past few years, he'd stayed away from Eaglecrest, the Delgado family ranch, as much as he could. Of course, he kept busy on the rodeo circuit, but still.

Before she knew it, she was seated across from him with Lauren and James beside her. The guys greeted each other with little beyond grunts and nods while Lauren and Denae exploded into conversation.

"Tori Carmichael. Long time no see." Sawyer leaned back in his seat and gave her a bold once-over, a slight smirk marring his handsome face.

She could only be thankful she was already seated, so his gaze couldn't linger on the hem of her skirt. She definitely hadn't dressed to impress *him*. "Hi, Sawyer."

"Looking good." He nodded approvingly. "Still working for your folks?"

Her chin came up just slightly. "Sure am. The Flying Horseshoe is a happening place. We've built several more guest cabins and are solidly booked up for most of the summer. Well into the fall, really."

"Ever thought of spreading your wings a little? Flapping your way out of the nest?"

She skewered him with a glare, but no impact was visible. "I happen to love horses, and I love people." With a few exceptions, like the irritating one across from her. "There isn't a more beautiful, peaceful spot on earth than my parents' ranch. My cabin sits beside a tranquil lake with glacier peaks in the distance. What more could I want?"

Sawyer grinned. "Bright lights. Excitement. Parties and dancing. There's adventure elsewhere. You should try it sometime."

She wrinkled her nose.

He leaned across the table. "I could show you."

"—isn't that right, Tori?"

Whew. A more timely interruption had never come. She turned to Denae. "What's that?"

"Garret doesn't even need to think about what his hands are doing."

"Umm..."

Denae laughed. "Playing piano. It's like he gets a glimmer of an idea and then his fingers just do it."

"He's very talented." Didn't they all know this already? Why was this a topic she needed to weigh in on? Not that she wasn't thankful to break from Sawyer.

"And he can pick up nearly any other instrument, too. Flute, guitar, clarinet."

"Probably four years of music school didn't hurt," James put in.

Tori swiveled to stare at her brother. "Really?" How little she actually knew Garret. Where had he even lived before moving here? What were his life experiences? Did the guy think about anything besides music and horses?

She had no clue.

"Where did he go to college?" asked Denae.

James shrugged. "He didn't say, but he's been playing since he was a kid. That's all I really know."

"I could never stand up in front of a crowd and sing." Sawyer smirked.

Tori stifled her eye-roll.

Lauren laughed. "For you, it's all about the eight-second ride. Because no one is staring at you that whole time."

He smirked and winked at Tori. "Of course, they are. And I'll give them the show they're looking for."

How could he even stand himself?

CHAPTER 3

G arret parked beside Trevor's big, black pickup and wiped his palms down his jeans before exiting. Why was he nervous? No reason. This was just the gang, all the friends who'd made room for a newcomer five years ago.

The aromas of steak, fried onions, and baked potatoes enclosed him as he entered the restaurant, mingled as they were with beer and fried chicken. George Strait crooned from the speakers, nearly drowning out the chatter and laughter. Wait staff in jeans, snap-front plaid shirts, and cowboy hats worked the crowded tables.

His friends were at their usual booth in the middle of the space. His gaze zeroed right in on Sawyer Delgado. The youngest of the three brothers was rarely home, and it seemed a bit early for him to arrive for Trevor and Denae's wedding. How often did he get a break from the rodeo circuit? An unfamiliar woman sat across from him, holding his total attention. Maybe he'd come to introduce his newest girlfriend to his family.

The newcomer turned toward Lauren beside her. Garret caught her profile and stumbled to a stop in the middle of the restaurant. Tori Carmichael, with short reddish hair? Since when? He'd seen her in church a few days back with brown hair past her shoulders. What was she—

An elbow caught him from behind.

"Sorry." Garret stepped aside and let the other group pass. He'd blocked the corridor while he stared. It wasn't that he cared what Tori did with her hair... although why crop it short? He'd just been caught off guard, that was all.

Also, seeing Sawyer flirt with her assured Garret he'd rather enter the booth from this end, not the far one. The farthest possible from the pair of them and, no, there was no need to analyze that random thought.

He put his hand on the back of the padded bench beside James. "Scoot over, why don't you?"

"Over here." Across the table, Denae patted the seat beside her. She'd already shifted closer to Trevor, pushing her fiancé toward Sawyer.

"I—" How could he explain he didn't want to sit where he'd be forced to look at Tori? But it would be just as bad watching Sawyer's animated face as he talked to her. Either side, he was the fourth on the bench, crowding the others a little. "Anyone else coming?"

Denae shook her head. "Carmen said they couldn't make it, as Uncle Howard is feeling poorly. And Cheri and Kade are tied up with her grandparents this evening."

"I see." He settled into the seat beside her, and she scooted closer to Trevor. Maybe that was her game plan.

Only, Trevor elbowed Sawyer, who made a production like he was about to fall off the bench. This was crazy. There was plenty of room for four, even if three of them were broad-shouldered cowboys. Denae barely took up any space at all.

"I know when I'm not wanted." Sawyer laughed, rounded the end, and nudged Tori over.

A blush surged up her cheeks, and she shot a quick glance toward Garret. What, to be sure he noticed Sawyer had a crush on her? Maybe it was mutual. They'd have plenty of time to explore that as partners for the upcoming wedding. That would be good, right?

"Can I get you guys some drinks?" Their waitress appeared at the other end of the table, pen and notepad in hand. "Coke for you, Trevor?"

"Yes, please," said Trevor. "Denae?"

"Ice water for me. Thanks, Anna."

The waitress grinned. "And hold the lemon. Got it."

Garret asked for a ginger ale then the orders wrapped around the other side of the table, ending with Sawyer.

"Wait, you all know this gorgeous woman?" The rodeo star gestured around the group then looked up at Anna. He rose to his feet, clutched his hat over his heart, and took her hand. "I'm Sawyer Delgado, and I don't believe we've met."

"You must be Trevor and Kade's brother." She chuckled. "I'm Anna Winter... ready to take your order."

Still holding Anna's hand, Sawyer turned to Trevor. "Tell me she's invited to your wedding."

Denae giggled. "Of course, she is. Anna's one of our friends."

"Save me a dance or five." Sawyer batted his eyelashes at her.

Seriously?

Anna tugged her hand free, but she was still grinning. "You're not a bit shy, are you?"

Sawyer gave a slight bow. "Life's too short."

Once, Garret might have made a show of gagging on the other guy's over-the-top flirtation, but tonight he didn't have it in him. How could Sawyer switch from one woman to another in the blink of an eye? Five seconds ago he'd been stringing Tori along, and now he'd totally switched gears.

Tori stared down at her hands, probably from humiliation. It just wasn't right what Sawyer was doing to her.

"I'll get your drinks and be back for your orders in a couple of minutes." Anna's gaze swept Sawyer before she strode away.

"Slow down, dude." Trevor leaned across the table. "She's a nice girl, not someone for you to add to your string of conquests."

Sawyer slouched in his seat and slid his arm along the top of the bench behind Tori. "Not all of us are as stick-in-the-mud as you are, bro." He waggled his eyebrows at Denae. "Although *she's* loosened you up a bit. Good thing."

This had been planned as a comfortable dinner with friends. Things had changed.

"How long are you in town, Sawyer?" Lauren leaned around Tori to see him.

"I've got a rodeo down Bozeman way on the weekend. I'll be back for the wedding."

"Figuring on retiring someday soon?" asked James.

Sawyer shook his head. "I'm so close to the top of the charts I can almost taste the championship."

"It's not like you need more money," growled Trevor. "When is enough, enough?"

"It's not about greenbacks. It's about glory. You wouldn't understand."

Garret held his breath, but Trevor just leaned back and studied his brother with no visible reaction. "There's more to life than either of those. We could sure use you riding range."

Sawyer rolled his eyes. "Don't even talk to me about it. You've spent your entire existence hiding out at Eaglecrest. Kudos to your fiancée for seeing anything worthwhile in you and hauling you out of your self-imposed exile. Because, look! Here you are in a public place with people all around you. Amazing."

Garret could see the tic starting in Trevor's jaw, but his friend remained silent.

"You know what?" Sawyer surged to his feet. "Thanks for the dinner invite, but there's something I'd rather do with my time." His eyes scanned faces around the table, lingering for a second on Tori. "I'm just going to see what time that hot waitress gets off work and go find dinner elsewhere. Takeout from Izzie's Pizza sounds mighty fine at the moment."

The relief at the table was nearly tangible as Sawyer swaggered off. He talked to Anna near the door for a minute then, grinning, tugged the brim of her hat in a familiar gesture before leaving.

Garret let out a long whoosh of air as the door swung closed behind the rodeo star. "Well, that was interesting."

Trevor shook his head. "Sorry for inviting him in the first place. He stopped by the house just as I was ready to leave, and the offer just popped out."

"It's fine," assured James. "I only hope Anna is smart enough not to be taken in by him."

Tori shot her brother a quick glance.

"He's usually more easy-going," Denae protested. "Something must have happened to get him in a snit like that. You couldn't have known."

But Garret was watching Tori's reaction. Surely she knew to avoid a player like Sawyer Delgado, especially when he'd made no bones about flirting with Anna while sitting next to her.

Garret wanted her to find some nice guy to date so she'd quit giving him those sidelong gazes. But she needed to find a *nice* guy, and that was definitely not Sawyer.

It wasn't Garret, either.

STUPID SAWYER.

Tori should've known getting all dolled up for a dinner out with the gang would backfire. Who knew Trevor and Kade's bronc-riding brother would be home and tag along? Never mind that he'd actually notice Tori as a woman for the first time. Sure, they'd played together as kids, but hadn't really remained friends as teens. Now they'd been thrown together for the upcoming wedding. He and Trevor might not be close, but they *were* brothers.

It was more that Garret likely made assumptions about how well she and Sawyer knew each other, though maybe Sawyer had put that to rest with his blatant flirtation with Anna.

Tori gritted her teeth. And now Garret visited at the other end of the table while she sat with an invisibility cloak wrapped around her.

Sorry, mouthed Denae with a moue of disappointment from her spot between Trevor and Garret.

Tori shrugged and flicked her eyebrows. Had she really thought a simple makeover would lure Garret in? If he were that shallow, she didn't want him, anyway. Right? A lot more went on behind his watchful eyes, though. He came across naive — gullible, even — but she was pretty sure that was a role he played, not the real cowboy. How was she supposed to get behind the facade and learn who he really was?

Maybe it wasn't her mission. Maybe he'd be a disappointment. Maybe he was in witness protection hiding out in their sleepy town. Or worse, his elderly parents were really his captives, and the riding stables a coverup for illicit operations. She stifled a giggle, but not quickly enough.

Lauren leaned closer. "What's so funny?"

Tori shook her head. "Nothing. Just a random thought." She shot a quick glance at Garret. He leaned casually against the padded bench, hat tilted back, grinning at something James had said.

A really stupid random thought. He was far too sweet

and easy-going. Whatever he was hiding, it wasn't anything sinister.

But what guy their age didn't seem to have any ambition? She couldn't go by college degrees — they weren't that common here. Her brother had been in his second year of business school when Dad's accident had brought him home to take over management of the ranch. Trevor had taken some agriculture courses at the community college and followed up to get his degree online. Spencer Haviland was an accountant, but then he hadn't grown up here.

Neither had Garret.

She glanced at him again. This time his gaze bounced off hers before he refocused on Lauren.

Denae turned to Garret. "So, you're the last guy standing in this bunch. We should get Lauren to turn her matchmaking skills on y—"

"Hey!" protested Lauren. "It wasn't like that."

Denae's grin glittered. "No, you're right. You were busy trying to avoid James, and look where that got you."

Tori willed her friends not to include her in this conversation. She'd seen how Lauren's ploy to get James dating someone else had nearly backfired, even though everyone had plainly seen the two of them were meant for each other. Surely her own infatuation with Garret was much less visible. Although, Denae knew. Tori sent a beseeching look at her friend. *Keep me out of this.*

Denae smirked then turned back to Garret. "There are plenty of single women in this town."

Don't name names.

He glanced coolly at Denae and shrugged. "You may

as well save yourself the effort. I'm not planning to ever get married."

Tori's heart stuttered. Why would he say such a thing? Didn't everyone want to settle down and have a family? She sure did. With him.

Trevor leaned past his bride-to-be to offer his friend a lopsided grin. "I said the same thing."

"And our wedding is in nine days." Denae smiled softly up at him.

He nuzzled her hair. "There's never been a happier goner."

Aw. They were so sappy it was adorable. Why did Garret refuse to look at her that way? For once, Tori let her gaze linger. His sandy curls peeked from beneath his cowboy hat, and his perfectly stubbled jaw was angular and strong. The guy was so gorgeous he removed all oxygen from the atmosphere.

His blue eyes focused on hers and held for a few seconds before he looked away. There'd been nothing to see there. No flicker of awareness, no amusement or disdain. Nothing at all.

Tori jabbed at the last few scraps of romaine and dragged them through a smear of guacamole. The taco salad didn't seem to have as much flavor as usual.

Garret had polished off a twelve-ounce steak, a Caesar salad, and a ginormous baked potato drowning in butter, sour cream, and real bacon bits, all while creating a playlist for church next Sunday with James's input.

"Anyone for dessert?" Anna topped off the guys' coffee cups.

Garret nodded. "Cherry pie and ice cream, please."

"Make that two," added James.

"Three," said Trevor.

Denae raised both hands and shook her head. "No thanks."

"Toffee pudding for me," said Lauren.

Tori grimaced. Usually she'd totally be up for the restaurant's signature dessert, but not tonight. No need to spend money on more tasteless food she didn't need. "Not tonight."

"All right then." Anna flashed a smile.

"I hope my brother didn't offend you too badly." Trevor studied the waitress.

"Not at all. He seems like a fun guy."

"Fun is all he thinks about." There was an unspoken warning in Trevor's words.

Anna grinned. "No worries. I can handle myself. I'll be right back with your desserts." She hustled off, her boots clacking on the wood floor.

Trevor grimaced. "I tried."

"Anything between them won't last more than five minutes, anyway." Lauren wiped condensation off the side of her diet cola with a finger. "Anna dresses western because that's the uniform at The Branding Iron, but she doesn't ride. Sawyer thinks of nothing but rodeo."

And his ego. But Tori didn't say it.

For some reason Garret sat watching her, like she cared what Sawyer did or didn't do. What, because the guy had flirted with her? Tori raised her chin and looked straight back at Garret.

He shifted to focus on James.

Whatever that was about. For a few seconds here and

there, something seemed to pass between her and Garret, but then he shuttered his face, time and time again, and blocked her right out. He might as well hide behind a medieval castle wall, complete with moat and drawbridge, for all the chance she had.

But... why? What was wrong with her that a man this amazing found her distasteful? If only she knew.

CHAPTER 4

G arret? You home?"

His mother's voice sounded weak, and he frowned as he strode through the house to her studio toward the back. "Mom?" He found her huddled under a blanket in her easy chair, though it didn't seem cold in here. "You okay?"

She blinked up at him as he flicked on a reading lamp. "I don't feel so well."

He knelt beside her and wrapped her hands in his as he searched her face. "What kind of not well?"

"It's probably nothing. Just a summer flu."

"Where's Dad?"

Mom squeezed Garret's hands. "Gone off to bed already. He was pretty tired after helping the farrier all day, but I wanted to wait up for you."

She made it sound like it was the wee hours, but it was barely ten. But they'd always been early-to-bed, early-to-rise people as far back as he could remember.

"Can I fix you a cup of tea or get you a snack?" So

long as it didn't require him actually cooking. "Have you taken anything for the fever?"

Her trembling hand touched her forehead. "I have a fever?"

"You feel a little warm. Maybe it's just because you're all bundled up."

"Tea would be nice, but I can make it."

"Or you could let me do something for you for a change." Garret didn't often let himself get sentimental, but he owed this woman everything.

"I can do it." Mom pushed against his hands as she struggled to stand. "Let's go in the kitchen."

Garret followed her. She seemed steady enough, though so slight it seemed even a breath of air might topple her. She'd be seventy-three this summer. How would he handle it when she or Dad passed on? Even at the thought, a chill passed over him.

He pulled out a chair at the table. "Here, sit. I may not be able to cook, but I can boil water. What kind of tea would you like?"

"Chamomile, at this time of night." She skirted the chair and headed for the fridge. "Would you like a bowl of soup?"

"I just finished a steak dinner at The Branding Iron." It had been only an hour since he'd had the last bite of the cherry pie that followed, and he'd be stuffed until morning.

"Oh." She peered into the fridge then removed a container of the hamburger soup they'd been eating all week.

It wasn't bad, but enough was enough. Didn't she

used to have a larger repertoire of recipes? Garret watched her trembling hands scrape the contents into a small saucepan — no microwave for *her* — and set it on a front element as he filled the kettle from the tap.

"I'll get it from here." He turned her toward the vinyl-covered chair by the table.

She didn't protest as she sank onto the seat. "Thanks, son."

Garret pulled two cups from the cupboard, dumped a teabag in each of them, then gave the soup a stir while he kept a surreptitious eye on his mother. "Maybe you should teach me to cook," he said at last. Not that he'd ever been particularly interested. Still wasn't, but he did like to eat.

Mom shook her head. "You need to find some pretty girl who can take care of you."

Been there. Done that. "Lots of guys my age can cook. We're supposed to be self-sufficient, not dependent on someone else to do everything for us."

"She won't do everything, of course. She'll take care of your home and your children."

Garret pushed aside his memories and raised his eyebrows at her. "You do know a lot of women in my generation have careers. Lauren Carmichael is still a full-time veterinarian, even though she's married to James."

She frowned. "Maybe that will change when they have children."

"Not everyone wants to have kids. Not everyone *can*." Oops. He shouldn't have said that. Shouldn't have reminded her. He turned off the soup and poured boiling water over the teabags.

"We wanted babies," Mom said softly. "But I'm glad God gave you and Kellen to us."

And the dozen foster kids that had come and gone. "Have you heard from him?"

A shadow crossed her face as she closed her eyes. "I'd tell you."

He knew she would. Speaking of his older brother — adopted from different situations, but still brothers — was all but taboo. Unlike Garret, Kellen had chafed under the Morrisons' rules. He'd drifted into a life of drugs and alcohol as a teen and hadn't been heard from in years. Who knew if he was even still alive?

Drugs were no temptation to Garret. He'd seen first-hand what they did to a person. He squeezed his eyes shut, willing away the memory of his mother's lifeless, wasted body. She'd been the second person to leave him — his father had been first — but her death had set the pattern for his life.

He'd thought he could break it, but he'd been proven wrong. Everyone left, either by death or more creatively. That's just how it was. Sooner or later, Tuck and Nancy Morrison would leave him, too. They wouldn't do it on purpose like some others had, but the result would be the same. He'd be alone, this time for the remainder of his life.

So, yeah. It was probably time to learn how to cook.

Tori swung a saddle to Coaldust's back. The gelding

shifted away, but she knew his tricks and moved with him to settle the tack in place. "Easy, boy."

His ears flicked, and she rubbed his velvety nose before looping the end of the cinch strap through the D-ring and tightening it.

"I've got Pippi and Domi saddled and in the corral," came Tori's sister's voice from the alley. "Off to get Luna."

"Thanks." Tori straightened. "I'm glad you're coming on the trail ride today. Seems like I never get to see you."

"I feel like I never get to ride! When Dad offered to keep the kids, I jumped at it." Meg shook her head. "I only hope he's up for it. Sophia is into everything these days."

"Aiden will do whatever running Dad needs," Tori called after her. "They'll be fine."

Their father had suffered a debilitating accident nearly a decade back when some moron had flipped the switch on a piece of farm equipment while Dad was trying to clear the auger. His legs had been caught and mangled. He was lucky to have survived.

It had been a near thing, changing the lives of everyone in the family. James had come home from college and shouldered the responsibility of the man of the house, and he and Mom had devised the plan to transition the Flying Horseshoe from a working ranch to a ranch resort. They'd used insurance money to build the first few guest cabins.

Meg, the second-born, had taken the opportunity to indulge her wild streak. She'd pretty much gone off the deep end for a few years. Thank the Lord — and Eli

Thornton — she'd eventually come to her senses. Eli adored Meg and had married her, stepping in to be Aiden's daddy. Sophia Grace had joined the family two years back. Meg had done everything wrong, yet somehow landed on her feet, restored and forgiven.

Tori had little in common with her sister. Like James, she couldn't imagine purposefully hurting her gentle parents or bucking their plans for her. Sure, she'd once dreamed of heading off to college to become a teacher, but she'd still been in high school when everything changed.

Now, she taught kids and adults to ride the mountain trails, taught them western lore, including plant and animal identification. She'd been telling herself her time would come, but she was beginning to wonder if her dream was only a mirage. Twenty-seven years old and still working for her parents. She'd managed to escape as far as moving into the end guest cabin after James vacated it for his and Lauren's new house.

Unlike her siblings, the Flying Horseshoe was the only life she'd ever known. She'd drifted into it, first from family need, then from lack of anything to jolt her out of her rut.

But, now, Dad was stable. The Flying Horseshoe had found its place as a tourist destination. They didn't need her anymore. Any hired hand could do what she did.

The clopping of horse hooves roused Tori, and she grabbed Coaldust's reins and led him out of his stall toward the corral. He tossed his head at the sight of Luna, being led by Meg, but stayed settled.

Meg laughed. "He's ready for a good run."

"He sure is. Is today's group up for it?"

"Supposed to be intermediate to advanced riders, so here's hoping."

Tori scanned the group milling around just outside the corral.

Several young teen boys with shiny new cowboy hats watched eagerly from atop the rails. One pointed at Coaldust. "Can I ride that one?"

"No, sorry." Tori smiled to soften the sting. "He's mine."

He and his buddy elbowed each other. "I could handle him."

"Possibly, but you won't get the chance." She stared him full in the eye. "He's off limits to guests."

"Aw, lady..."

She hooked Coaldust's reins to a post in the middle, out of easy reach. She and Meg still needed to grab two more horses before they could get this group on the trail. She had half a mind to assign the kid to Aiden's mount, Nellie. It would serve him right to put him on a geriatric mare suitable for a six-year-old.

Nah, he was just trying to impress his friends with his bravado. So long as he didn't get carried away with it, they'd all be fine.

"I've got Snowball," said Meg as they returned for the last two.

Tori nodded. That left her with Tawny, a docile mare that picked up her pace only when the herd did. They returned a few minutes later to find James leaning on the fence next to the boys. She breathed a sigh of relief.

"Are you a real cowboy?" asked the kid in wonder.

James angled a glance at him. "Your name's Ryan, right?"

The boy nodded eagerly.

"Guess it depends on what you think a real cowboy is, Ryan. I live on a ranch, I've got my own horse, and I ride nearly every day."

"Do you rope calves? Brand them?"

"I've done it. I still get in on roundup with friends at a nearby ranch, but we don't raise calves on the Flying Horseshoe anymore."

"Why not?"

James chuckled. "No cows."

"Then it's not a real ranch, and you're not a real cowboy."

James tipped his hat. "Whatever you say." He met Tori's gaze across Tawny's back with a little smirk. "Ready to mount up? Ollie sent over the saddlebags containing lunch."

Tori nodded. "Okay, everyone." She pulled her phone out of her pocket to look at the list of guests who'd signed up for this ride. "I'll assign horses first. No trading." She eyed Ryan. "I'll be taking the lead, then you'll follow in single file. My sister, Meg, will take the rear." She pointed to the path around the lake. "We'll be taking that trail back up the valley there, and we'll stop for lunch at a breath-taking waterfall before continuing a bit further. And we'll be back to the ranch in time for supper. Any questions?"

Ryan's hand shot up.

"Yes, Ryan?"

"Which horse is mine?"

"I'll get to you in a minute." Tori scanned the group gathered against the rails. Thankfully most were older teens and adults, including a couple of men who looked to be in their forties. Hopefully one of them was Ryan's dad.

Behind her, James clipped the padded bags to the back of Coaldust's saddle.

"Okay, then." She glanced at the list. "Drake Jones, you'll be on Domi. Come on through the gate, and Meg will introduce you. Colin, you'll be on Luna. James will give you a hand."

Ryan's buddy hopped over the fence, a big grin on his face.

"Aw, man, I wanted that horse," mumbled Ryan. "She'll probably give me some old nag."

Some days Tori couldn't remember why she'd wanted to be a teacher, but it had been Ms. Sorenson who'd piqued her interest in biology in seventh grade. An interested teacher at that vital age could make all the difference. So, as much as she felt like putting Ryan in his place, she'd resist.

"Want me to get Nellie?" Meg murmured.

"Such a temptation, but no. I'll put him on Snowball. It'll be fine."

"If you say so."

It took a few more minutes for all the guests to be mounted up, stirrups adjusted, and questions answered, and then James swung open the corral gate. "Have fun, everyone! Ollie's got a heap of ribs in the smoker today, and they'll be waiting for you on your return."

Tori led the group past her brother. "I've got my mobile phone," she assured him.

"Good to know. Hopefully you won't need it. You and Meg will be fine."

Of course, they would. Tori had been leading groups into the back country for the past seven years. She'd only had to call for help a couple of times.

"How fast can we go?" Ryan nudged Snowball up beside her before they'd even reached the lakeside kayak rack.

Tori closed her eyes for a second, took a deep breath, and forced a smile for the boy. "As fast as Coaldust and I allow. We'll be in single file, remember? And no passing."

"Aw, man, it's like a sissy ride."

"Prove you can handle Snowball, and you can try some jumping in the arena later. She loves to jump."

The boy's face brightened. "Really?"

"Sure. But I need you to prove you're a good listener. Not just to me, but to Snowball."

"Yes, ma'am. I will."

Crisis averted. Hopefully.

CHAPTER 5

Time on the trails above the riding stables had cleared Garret's mind. He checked over his shoulder once more to see Cocoa plodding behind him and Trudy. The brown mare hated being ponied along, but on days like today, leading another was the only way Garret could get a decent ride in himself while still seeing to the exercise needs of other horses in the stable. He and Trudy had both been cooped up too much lately. All the horses had. He couldn't even remember the last time he'd made it to the trapper's cabin back in the mountains.

He rounded the last bend in the trail and Canyon Crossing Stables came into view. His heart swelled with pride. The ranch was tidy and neat with classic white board fences crisscrossing the green, rolling bench-land above the creek. The three main buildings — house, arena, and stables — formed a U at the end of the drive. Noah Cavanagh's truck sat close to the corral for the second day, with the farrier hard at work on Boomerang's hooves.

Garret had work to do, too. He nudged Trudy into a trot, and the lead rope tightened for a second before Cocoa decided to cooperate.

An old gray minivan turned into the drive. Seriously? Noela Bergstrom had uncanny timing, putting off riding Cocoa for days on end then showing up when Garret'd had enough.

She swung out, her three boys tumbling out of the van's side door, and stood watching his approach with her hands on her hips.

Like it was his fault she hadn't let him know she was coming — not that he'd have believed her, since something always came up. Garret dismounted at the stable doors.

"Cocoa," Noela crooned, rubbing the mare's face. Of course, Cocoa leaned into the caress.

"Didn't know you were coming today." Garret kept his voice mild.

"Dougie wanted to ride."

He glanced at the ten-year-old. "Still can. I've worked the kinks out of her. She was mighty restless earlier."

"I'll grab her tack." Noela pointed at the fence and skewered her boys with a look. "You three wait right here and don't move an inch."

"What's that guy doing?" Darren, the middle boy, pointed at Noah's mobile forge.

"Shoeing Boomerang," said Garret. "Noah is a farrier who comes every six weeks or so to take care of all the horses' feet."

"Even Cocoa?"

"Yep. It's part of the deal when you board a horse at Canyon Crossing." Their website called it spa treatment. The previous owners had left it up to the individual owners, but Garret's dad had quickly seen that led to haphazard care and more veterinary calls. They'd upped the board per horse and rolled the service in.

"Is that why it costs so much?" asked Dougie. "Mom says we might have to sell Cocoa."

Noela parked her saddle on a rack by the corral rails. "You talk too much, Dougie. Take Cocoa's lead from Garret and bring her over here."

The kid rolled his eyes but did as he was told. Noela made quick work of tacking up then adjusted the stirrups to fit her son before boosting him into the saddle. She opened the gate into the arena and slapped Cocoa's rump as Dougie rode past.

"Can I watch that guy?" Darren wanted to know, still eyeing Noah.

"If you sit on the fence beside my dad and don't get in the way."

"That old guy's your dad?" Davey, the youngest brother, asked. "I don't have a dad. He died."

Garret knew how that felt, but he hadn't bothered to let anyone in Saddle Springs know his family dynamics. "Yup. Come with me." He boosted the two boys up on the top rail and introduced them to his father.

Noah glanced over. "Curious what I'm doing?"

"Yeah." Darren peered over. "But I'm too far away to see."

The farrier chuckled. "That's a good distance. You

make sure to let me or Mr. Morrison know if you need down, okay?"

Darren sighed. "Okay."

Garret headed back to Trudy, who stood patiently waiting for him. He led her into her box stall before removing her tack.

"Hey." Noela's voice came from the door.

He glanced over as he reached for the curry comb. "How's it going?" She'd be full of tales of woe, he was sure of that.

"I was meaning to talk to you about Cocoa, but Dougie spilled the beans."

"So you are thinking of selling?"

"I hate to." She grimaced. "Life is so crazy. The boys are in every sport known to mankind and, with the weird hours I can pick up at Manahan's, it seems we're always racing around. Cocoa is getting the short end of the stick."

He leaned an arm over Trudy's back and studied her. "You're good with horses."

"I love them. I miss riding so much. It's one of the things Jay and I did together all the time and even with the boys when they were all small enough to ride with us. He'd put Davey in a carrier on his back and Dougie in front of him."

Garret had met Jay a few times before his untimely death. A logger, he'd been killed by a rogue tree coming down. "I'm sorry."

"It's not on you. But... I'm just not sure what to do. Would you buy her from me?"

He shook his head. "I don't need another horse, but

you could try the Rocking H. Last I heard, Spencer Haviland was looking for another mount or two."

"They live so far from town, I'd never get to see her."

"Well, isn't that the point? When you sell something, it belongs to the buyer."

Noela rolled her eyes. "I know that, Garret. But I'm not sure I want such a drastic solution. Maybe I could lease her to the Flying Horseshoe. Do you know if they're looking for horses for tourists to ride?"

"Not a clue." And he didn't want to speculate, not when he'd spent his entire ride writing music in his head to avoid thinking about certain hazel eyes.

Something poked at the back of his mind. "What do you do with the boys while you work?"

"Jay's parents watch them. They wish the hours didn't shift around so much — I mean, they know it's not my fault, but still — but they appreciate bonding with their grandsons."

"You're good with horses."

Noela blinked. "Uh, yes? They've been part of my life since I was a kid."

"I should probably talk to my dad first..." But why? Garret shook his head. "Or not. Listen, we could sure use some help around here on a regular basis. As little as two or three hours a day would make an immense difference, but honestly? We could pay someone for six hours a day. Thirty hours a week. Interested?"

She stared at him. "Are you serious?"

"Totally. With Dad's declining health, he can't do as much as he used to." Garret poked his thumb in the direction of the farrier's truck. "To be honest, that right there is about his level these days. Keeping the flow of horses to Noah and talking the poor guy's ear off while he attends their hooves. Dad can hardly get into the saddle and, when he does, he can only manage a few minutes of riding. Then, when he's dismounted, he's done for the day and needs a heating pad and some painkillers."

"I had no idea."

"He probably wouldn't want word getting out. But it leaves more and more of the work to me every day. That's all the cleaning, all the exercising, all the health management, all the repairs, everything." Five years ago, Garret had been Tuck's assistant. He hadn't realized how much things had shifted until right now. Talking to Noela was not precipitous. It was necessary.

"So you're seriously offering me a job. A real one, with regular hours, not out of pity."

"Why would I pity you? Because you're widowed? I'm sorry about that, of course, and I can only guess the stress of raising three kids alone. But I also see how hard you work and how adjusted the boys seem to be. If you want a job, you've got it. You can even set your own hours." He turned back to Trudy, running the brush down her flank. "Pray about it, and let me know."

"Garret?"

"Hmm?" He glanced over. Oh, man, tears welled in her eyes. Way to make a guy uncomfortable.

"Thanks. I'll talk to Jay's folks and come back to you with available hours. Is that okay?"

"More than."

"I should go rescue your dad from Darren and Davey."

Good idea. And rescue Garret from chitchat. Would anyone think there was something between him and Noela because he hired her? Even though she probably had five or ten years on him?

Would Tori think that?

Not that Tori's opinion mattered. He hummed his new tune loudly while he curried Trudy, but it didn't completely block his thoughts.

"MAN, you are a thousand times more patient with those kids than I am." Meg removed Domi's tack and began to brush him.

"Ryan's a good kid. Most of them are. They just need to be heard."

"I like my own kids just fine. It's other people's kids I'm not so fond of."

Tori laughed. "Just wait until Aiden's that age."

"Spare me."

"And then Sophia. She's just like you, Meggie. You and Eli are going to be in *so* much trouble."

Meg made a face. "How come you never went crazy like I did?"

Tori lifted off Snowball's saddle, and Matt came to tote it to the tack room. She reached for the curry comb. "My question is the reverse. How come you went crazy, when we had the best parents and best examples in the world?"

"Million dollar question, I guess. Somehow it didn't seem enough. Too boring. Too... safe."

"I like safe." Sometimes it seemed she liked it too much. Was it time to shake things up? Step out of her comfort zone? "I've been thinking of becoming a teacher."

Meg paused and looked over. "You'd be good at that. Especially junior high."

"You think?" Kids Ryan's age presented a big challenge, but she loved the way they were still vulnerable children wobbling back and forth into maturity. It was definitely a time of life when a steadfast adult who believed in them could make a big difference.

"Yeah, I do."

"Aren't you going to tell me how much you'd miss me if I left the Flying Horseshoe?"

Meg shrugged. "I hadn't thought of it that way, honestly. Most kids do eventually leave home. Except in ranching communities, lots of times they settle a long way from their parents. But, yeah, I'd miss you."

"Wow, tell me how much I mean to you."

"Just giving the facts. Dad and Mom have Eli and me and James to help run the ranch. And Ollie and the staff."

Of course, Meg wouldn't consider Lauren part of the family business, since she still worked out of the veterinary clinic.

"Yeah, well. I'm looking into it." But college was a last resort. First she'd make another solid effort at catching Garret's eye. Why did he refuse to notice her? What could she do about it?

She'd think of something.

CHAPTER 6

G arret sat at the grand piano, his fingers warming up as they danced across the keyboard. Voices and laughter from the foyer warned him that the wedding party had arrived for the rehearsal. He wrenched his gaze away from the propped-open double doors and stared up at the sunset glow through the round stained glass window above the platform.

"New song?" James's voice came from over Garret's shoulder.

He startled, but his fingers kept playing. "Hey." What was he playing, anyway? Oh, the melody that had been coming to life in his mind over the past few days. "Uh, yeah. Just a song I'm writing."

"Lyrics?"

Hazel eyes with glints of green and brown and gold.
Gazing into the windows of your soul—

What? His hands dropped discordantly. How had he

even noticed Tori's eyes? Because the words were certainly not about anyone else.

"You okay?" James's eyebrows pulled together in concern.

"Fine." Garret glanced around.

Everyone stood still, staring at him with worry and concern etched on their faces.

"Really. It's all good." He launched into *Ode to Joy*, practicing for the processional. Avoiding his friends.

Pastor Roland came in from the side door, rubbing his hands together. "Everyone's here?"

Looked like it to Garret. Bride, groom, parents, wedding party, a few close friends.

"Let's gather together here at the front and ask God's blessing on this evening."

Garret didn't miss the roll of Sawyer's eyes or the way his arm draped loosely over Tori's shoulders as they drifted toward the platform in the midst of the group. He didn't miss the way Tori stiffened and shifted away, but not enough to dislodge the bronc rider's arm. He didn't miss the unease in his own gut at the sight.

No, Garret. Remember. Remember it's dangerous to get too close to people. Dangerous for them. Dangerous for you.

All he had to do was remember the wedding eight years ago. A small church in Kentucky. His glowing bride, her radiance so full of promise. And not two hours later, a crash that claimed Jenna's life. Destroyed his.

What had been left, Chantelle had demolished.

Tori wasn't like Chantelle, but it didn't matter. The common denominator of all disaster was Garret Morrison. He couldn't pursue Tori. One of them — and probably both — would face an unprecedented catastrophe, and that was unfair to her.

Not that she was likely interested in him, anyway.

But, as Pastor Roland said *amen*, their gazes tangled for a brief moment. Garret hadn't imagined anything. She was definitely aware of him... like he was of her. He forced his gaze back to the stained glass window as he began to play again. Music, his defense against everything.

GARRET ALWAYS SEEMED to hide behind his music.

For half a second, he'd seemed aware of her. It happened just often enough that Tori was sure it wasn't all in her imagination.

But then he looked away. Always. Why didn't he act on his attraction? What went on inside Garret Morrison's brain that kept him aloof?

Maybe it was her. Something was wrong with her. She wasn't pretty enough. Ambitious enough. Smart enough. Something... but what? She might not be as thin as Denae or as bubbly as Lauren or as composed as Cheri or as focused as Carmen, but she wasn't so terrible, was she?

"Ladies, please go to the ready room with Bonnie and, gentlemen, please come with me to the office. Garret, you've got a repertoire of songs to play as guests are being seated, correct?"

Garret nodded and switched to *Love So Amazing* with not so much as a transition.

"Ushers, please take your place at the back, ready to

escort guests to their seats. The last to be seated—" the pastor checked his notes "—will be Michelle Archibald, then Russ and Gloria Delgado then, finally, Lisa Williams."

Lisa, the bride's mom, cast a glare at her ex-husband's current wife, while Michelle twined her fingers with Stewy's, leaning into him without acknowledging Lisa. The divorce and remarriage had been more than twenty years ago, but it was only in the past year that the two women could be in the same room without altercations of some kind.

Every time, it reminded Tori how thankful she was that her own parents remained happily married. Dad's devastating accident had certainly been a trial for them, but they'd grown even closer, proving the 'in sickness and in health' part of their vows.

She wanted a marriage like theirs. She wanted it with Garret.

Tori pushed the thought away and followed the female contingent of the bridal party toward the back, Garret's music setting the tempo. Too bad her heart didn't feel like dancing.

"PIZZA'S HERE!" called Trevor's dad. "Come on into the fellowship hall and let's ask God's blessing on the remainder of this evening."

Garret followed the group of family and friends out of the sanctuary and down the corridor.

"Hey." James fell into step beside him. "You're kind of quiet tonight. Everything okay?"

"I'm fine." Garret found a smile and offered it to his friend. "There's just a lot going on out at Canyon Crossing with my parents' health and all."

James slowed. "What's happening?"

"I'm not sure. They are both far more tired than they used to be, and I'm concerned. Of course, they refuse to see the doctor."

"I'm guessing that means you've got a lot extra on your plate."

"Yeah. It will be okay, I'm sure. Just a hurdle right now."

"You can admit it's a problem, you know. Even ask for help."

Garret forced a laugh. "It's not that bad. Besides, you guys are in your busy season, too. Everyone is."

James stopped, blocking the doorway to the fellowship hall as he stared in Garret's eyes. "Friends do what needs to be done to help each other out. Give us the chance."

A great thought, and one he could see Tori's brother believing. It's how the Carmichaels and Delgados and Havilands operated, for sure. But the Morrisons were still newcomers. They weren't woven into the fabric of Saddle Springs like the ranching families who'd settled Mustang County before the railroad opened the West.

"We need more than a temporary hand, to be honest." Garret looked past James's shoulder, his gaze colliding with Tori's. "I hired Noela Bergstrom to help out. She needed a job with steadier hours, and she's intuitive with horses. She's taking on some of the exercising and cleaning."

"Oh, good." James's face cleared as he stepped aside. "That will be a benefit to both parties."

"It will." Garret shifted to James's other side — away from Tori — as they walked toward the long table where boxes from Izzie's Pizza were laid out in a row with a giant bowl of Caesar salad next to paper plates and napkins at one end.

"This is where I bow out." Sawyer's voice.

Garret turned to see the rodeo star next to his dad.

Russ Delgado narrowed his gaze at his youngest son. "Please stick around. It's your brother's big day."

Sawyer shrugged. "That's tomorrow, and I'll be there. But tonight, I've got a hot date."

"Son..."

He held up both hands. "Sorry. Plans are made. Anna gets off work in ten minutes, and I promised to pick her up. Can't break a promise."

"I would've thought Anna'd seen through him by now," James murmured.

How was Tori taking this? Sawyer had been flirting with her all through the rehearsal itself. Garret glanced around only to find Tori had come up beside him. Too close. He managed not to shy away. "Guess your date is two-timing you."

She angled her head to look up at him with those sparkling hazel eyes. "He's not my date, just because we're paired for the ceremony. We didn't particularly get along when we were kids, and we still don't like each other."

"Uh..." *Eloquent, Garret.* "Well, at least you know where you stand."

"With him."

He blinked. What was that supposed to mean?

Before he realized her intentions, she'd tucked her hand around his elbow. "Want to get some pizza?"

Her fingernails were tipped in turquoise to match the floral dress that flared around her knees.

Hazel eyes with glints of green and brown and gold.

Gazing into the windows of your soul.

Everything you think is mirrored there—

No. It had just been an idle tune, not an ode to Tori's eyes. At least that's how it had started.

She tugged him into the lineup behind James and Lauren.

He should pull away. Think of something he needed to say to Trevor's brother Kade across the room. Say he wasn't hungry. Pretend he'd received a message from his mom.

Anything.

Instead, he shuffled forward, hyper aware of her touch on his arm, the brush of the back of her hand on his ribcage, the graze of her shoulder against his bicep. That entire side of his body buzzed, a little warmer than the other.

He hadn't been this aware of a woman since Chantelle. He stiffened, closed his eyes, and forced himself to relax.

Tori looked up at him. "You okay?"

Tori was not Chantelle. Nothing like her. She wasn't

sweet Jenna, either. But that didn't mean Garret should let down his guard. Not for Tori's sake. Not for his.

He sidled away just enough that her hand dropped. Instantly his body chilled, and it was all he could do not to shift back.

"Why do I make you uncomfortable?" came Tori's quiet voice as her eyes met his.

"Uh... sorry?" He pointed at the end of the table. In front of them, James picked up two plates and handed one to his wife. "Your turn."

"I can't figure you out."

"I'm the mystery man." Garret reached past Tori and offered her a plate. "There's no point in wasting too much time puzzling on it, honestly."

She stared at him a long moment before accepting the plate. "I can't decide if you're faking modesty, or what."

"There you go again," he said lightly. "Put your mind to better challenges, like what Sawyer Delgado is up to, or how world peace might be achieved."

Tori leaned closer. Heat flared up between them as she skewered him with her gaze. "I don't care what Sawyer Delgado is up to. He's a big boy and no concern of mine."

"World peace, then." Garret stepped around her and slid a slice of barbecue steak pizza to his plate. "This smells amazing."

"It does." Tori pressed against his arm. "I'd like one of those, too."

He knew a hint when he heard one, and served her. Was this how the remainder of the evening would play out, with her sticking to his side like a burr caught in a horse's mane? A burr didn't dislodge on its own. It tangled deeper and deeper until even a curry comb couldn't remove it. Only a sharp blade could.

Detailing his history to Tori would, no doubt, cut away her infatuation. He hated to do that. For one thing, he'd gone over five years locking a lid on his past and refusing to dwell on it. While he didn't know that Tori would tell anyone else, a secret like that was an unfair burden to place on her.

He really didn't want word getting out. He didn't want people's sympathy, nor did he want their speculation. Would they come to the same conclusion he had, that everything was his fault? Because, when everything else was stripped away, Garret Morrison was the common denominator of all the disasters in his life.

He couldn't inflict that on anyone as innocent as Tori. He *wouldn't*. She deserved better, a full life with a man who could love her and honor her as she was worthy of.

"Let's sit over there." She pointed to an empty table not far from the others.

Panic infused him, and he stopped in the middle of the open space. "I was planning to sit with James and Lauren."

Tori's shoulders drooped slightly. "You're seeing Noela, right?"

"Noela?" he repeated, sounding like an idiot to his own ears. "No. She works for me. Or she will, starting Monday."

"But you're interested in her."

"No. Not at all."

Tori shook her head. "I don't understand you."

Back to this, were they? "I'm not looking for a girl-friend or a wife, Tori. Not her. Not anyone." *Not even you.* But he couldn't say that out loud.

"But..." She searched his gaze. "Why?"

"It's a long story," he said lightly, "and one I don't feel like getting into tonight." Or at all, ever. "I'm joining James and Lauren now." He took a few steps, and yep, she stayed right with him.

"I'd like to hear your story. I don't know much about your life before your family bought Canyon Crossing."

"It's not that interesting." Garret set his plate on the table across from James. "Hey, guys."

Lauren's gaze toggled between Garret and Tori. "Hi there." The questions on her face were likely mirrored on most of the faces in the room, but he wasn't turning around to check.

"I'm grabbing some punch. Anyone else want some?"

"I'd like a glass." Tori set her plate in front of the chair beside his and flashed him a smile. "Thanks."

Yep, just like a burr tangled in a mane, she was proving awfully hard to dislodge.

CHAPTER 7

Tori's eyes stung with unshed tears as she witnessed Denae and Trevor pledging their lives to each other. From the angle where she stood between Lauren and Sadie, Denae's friend who'd come from Spokane to be the matron of honor, Tori couldn't see Denae's expression, but she could see Trevor's.

Quiet, taciturn Trevor Delgado's face was wreathed in a tender smile, his dark eyes filled with emotion as his hands clutched his bride's.

The sight stole Tori's breath. Oh, to be loved like Trevor loved Denae. To hear the man she loved boldly speak his wedding vows for all the world to hear.

Her gaze slid to the man on the piano bench where he observed those same promises. Something like longing glimmered on his face until his eyes shifted and connected with Tori's. Then the impassive mask she was so accustomed to seeing slid over him again, and his shoulders stiffened slightly.

"You may kiss your bride," Pastor Roland announced.

Trevor didn't need a second invitation. He cradled Denae's face between his hands and gave her a beautiful, tender kiss that had his bride clinging to his shoulders.

A rustle beside Tori pulled her attention away from the couple. Lauren made her way toward James and the grand piano. The couple picked up their microphones, and James nodded to Garret to begin the introduction to *When God Made You.* Then their voices melded in the beautiful lyrics by Newsong about Christian love. They were singing for the bride and groom, but the words were a touching testimony to their own eighteen-month-long marriage.

Tori tugged a tissue from the back of her bouquet and dabbed at her eyes, hoping her mascara wouldn't smudge. Her movement caught Garret's attention over at the piano, but his expression remained inscrutable.

The lyrics spoke of how God must have been thinking of the person when He made their partner, because they were so perfect for each other, like a dream come true.

Garret seemed perfect for Tori, too, but she was running out of patience. She'd been a bit forceful last night at rehearsal, but he'd still put her off. How much time was she going to give him? How much effort?

God?

But God wasn't answering. Not at the moment, anyway. The song came to a touching close as her brother and his wife gave each other a sweet smile before returning to their spots at either end of the wedding party. Garret segued into *The Love of God* as the pastor led Denae and Trevor through the candle-lighting ceremony, signifying two lives becoming one.

Pastor Roland turned to the audience. "It is my pleasure to introduce to you for the very first time, Mister and Missus Trevor and Denae Delgado!"

Cheers, clapping, and a few cat-calls erupted from the packed sanctuary as the newlyweds exchanged another quick kiss then made their way down the steps and down the aisle toward the back to the triumphant music pouring from the piano.

Beside Tori, Sadie moved to tuck her hand in the crook of Trevor's brother Kade's elbow. Then it was Tori's turn to meet Sawyer and, behind them, came Lauren and James.

They strode toward the foyer, and Sawyer leaned toward Tori's ear. "Well, he did it. Thought for sure he'd get cold feet and back out."

Tori shifted a half step away while keeping the pace. "Why would he? He loves her. That's plainly obvious."

Sawyer shrugged. "And now he's got a ball and chain wrapped around his ankle."

She jabbed him with her elbow, perhaps more forcefully than required. "That's not what marriage is."

"Yeah, well. From over here, that's what it looks like." Sawyer guided her into the receiving line beside Sadie and Kade then whispered in Tori's ear. "I mean, look at *this* poor sap. Kade didn't learn the first time. He's been married twice."

"Stop it. Your brother is very happy. Both of them are." The middle brother, Kade, had married his high school sweetheart two years back, then added a baby boy to their his-and-hers family. Tori angled a look up at Sawyer. "One day you'll fall in love. Then you'll see."

His eyebrows hiked up. "Are you declaring yourself to me, Ms. Carmichael?"

"Most definitely not. You are so not my type."

A slow grin creased his face. "I'm every woman's type."

"In your dreams."

"Well, I'm Anna's type. And she's not the first to think so... and probably not the last."

She cringed. Too much information. "How did you get so full of yourself?"

He shrugged, but the surge of chattering guests coming through the doors from the sanctuary diverted his attention.

Thankfully.

Tori shook hands with nearly two hundred people, many of them murmuring what a beautiful wedding it had been, but she was acutely aware of when the piano music stopped piping in via the speakers. She couldn't keep from watching for Garret in the thinning crowd. Her heart skipped a beat when she caught sight of him clapping Trevor on the back and giving Denae an awkward hug but, instead of shaking hands with the rest of the wedding party, he turned away and headed toward his parents waiting beside the door.

Tori's heart fell. He wouldn't even face her in the receiving line?

"Whew." Sawyer shook out his hand as though he'd been at it for days instead of minutes. "We need to get this show on the road."

She wouldn't let him bait her anymore. "Photos next."

He huffed a sigh, but his face brightened at the sight of Anna lingering near the window. She cast him a warm smile, and Sawyer elbowed Tori. "See what I mean? *She* thinks I'm hot."

Tori had always liked the waitress, but now? She just couldn't figure out what Anna saw in him.

Sawyer stepped out of line, but his dad intercepted his path. "We're all headed to the park by the bridge for photos now. You and Tori are riding with James and Lauren."

She could see his jaw tic from here. Well, she wasn't any more delighted with their pairing than he was, but they were doing it for Denae and Trevor, not their own pleasure. Seemed like Sawyer couldn't remember that for more than ten minutes at a time.

Anna fluttered her fingers at Sawyer and slipped out the door. How had he captured the Saddle Springs newcomer in one short week when Tori had been unable to make a dent in Garret's armor in five years?

She had photos to endure before the reception but then she'd find a way to make Garret dance with her.

"You okay, son?" Mom rested her hand on Garret's cheek in the church parking lot.

He forced a cheery smile. "I will be. Don't worry about me."

"I always will. I know how hard weddings are for you."

Garret opened the car door for her, and she slipped

inside while Dad clambered into the back. Both of them looked utterly done in from the brief excursion. He slid behind the wheel. "You two don't need to come to the reception if it's too much. Trevor and Denae will understand."

Mom shook her head slightly. "We'll come. It's our honor to be invited."

"We won't desert you, son," said Dad from behind him.

"You just say the word anytime then and I'll bring you home."

"I can still drive," Dad put in mildly.

"I'm just worried——"

"Not as worried as we are about you." Mom angled toward him. "Son, you need to allow your heart to open again. One day Dad and I will be gone, and I don't want to think of you alone and hurting for the rest of your life."

"I'll be fine." No, he wouldn't be. The thought of being truly on his own hovered like a dark cloud threatening to encompass him... but it wasn't as menacing as the thought of allowing someone inside his walls. Someone sweet and innocent like Tori. She'd run when she got a glimpse. He was only saving them both the heartache.

"You know we loved Jenna." Mom rested her hand lightly on his tuxedo sleeve as he drove through Saddle Springs toward the riding stable. "She was a ray of sunshine, and I'm so sorry for the terrible accident that took her from you."

Dad cleared his throat. "We weren't quite so fond of Chantelle."

Yeah, Garret knew that. He'd been stubborn, like that was anything new. But that time he'd been blind at the same time, ignoring the hints that she was using him, using the music he'd composed, using her inside track to snag that position with an upcoming Christian rock band right from under his nose. With his own music.

Meanwhile, he'd thought they had something special between them. She made him forget about Jenna for entire hours at a time. Forget that he was marked for pain and loneliness. He'd walked right into that one.

"We were so distressed about Chantelle," Mom went on. "It was a hard lesson for such a trusting soul."

Ha. Is that what Nancy Morrison thought of him? Trusting? No, that had been shattered long before. The little boy who'd watched his mother die had reached out too many times. Each time he'd come away with wounds, and the ones he'd suffer when Tuck and Nancy passed to their reward — and, oh, didn't they deserve that? — would be the final blow. He couldn't handle anymore.

"Son, what your mother is trying to say is to let love have a chance in your life. Remember Jesus came to give you life, abundant life."

"John 10:10," Mom replied, and Dad gave her a thumbs up.

Garret offered a shaky laugh. "Wow, you two are ganging up on me today."

"I'm sorry it seems that way," Mom said gently.

"Maybe that Noela girl you hired," suggested Dad.

"Those are good boys she's got, but they need a man's hand."

"Noela Bergstrom?" Mom's voice etched in disbelief as she swiveled to face Dad. "Are you kidding me? She's forty if she's a day."

"What does that matter?"

"She's not the right one for him. Now, think about Tori Carmichael—"

"No need to arrange a marriage for me." Garret's words might have erupted harsher than needed. He hadn't been prepared for the sight of her in a frothy pink dress with bare shoulders. "I'm perfectly content without a wife."

"But..."

"No buts, Mom." He turned into the drive at Canyon Crossing. "Now, we've got a couple of hours before we need to head over to the community center for the reception, so I suggest you have a snack and a nap so you'll be up for another outing later."

"A cup of tea does sound nice. Will you join us?"

"I don't think so. I'll shed the formalwear for a bit and take Trudy for a run. Could use some fresh air to clear my head."

"Don't forget what I said," she admonished him.

"I'll give it due consideration." Which would be all of eight seconds, just like a bronc rider. If only he could leap away from all thoughts of women and love as easily as Sawyer Delgado surged clear of flashing hooves... or charmed a pretty girl.

But Tori's hazel eyes insisted on dancing in front of

his mind, just like she'd insisted he save her a dance this evening.

If only he could bow out and skip the catered meal and dance altogether.

No. What he really wanted was to abandon his fears and dance with her a dozen times. But neither would happen. He needed to hold his persona like a cloak around him, aloof and disinterested.

It wasn't just himself he was protecting. It was also Tori.

CHAPTER 8

H i, Mrs. Morrison." Tori couldn't help it. She'd waited through the entire five-course dinner for a chance to escape the head table and find Garret. She'd promised him a dance, and she intended to make sure she got it.

"Why, hello, my dear." The older woman turned in her chair, her expertly applied makeup nearly masking the etched lines on her face. Her perfectly coifed hair and formal dress portrayed the elegant lady that she was. Mrs. Morrison pressed Tori's hands. "You look lovely today. Doesn't she, son?"

"As do you, Mrs. Morrison." No need to hold Garret at knifepoint. Tori leaned down to kiss the older woman's powdered cheek. "That shade of lilac is perfect for you."

"And you're so pretty in pink." Mrs. Morrison angled a look at her son on the other side of Tori. "Isn't she, Garret?"

Garret offered a smile that didn't reach his eyes as he

glanced at Tori. "Very pretty indeed. Would you like your sweater, Mom? It seems rather cool in here."

Ha. More like he'd been put on the spot and was trying to wiggle out of it. Tori turned to his dad. "Good evening, Mr. Morrison."

"Good evening, Victoria. It's good to see you."

What? No one called her by her full name, not since her parents had mostly given up trying to direct her life. Sometimes she felt so adrift she wished they'd start again.

Mrs. Morrison pressed a genteel hand to Garret's black tuxedo sleeve. "Oh, there's Fred Berkley. I wanted to speak with him and his dear wife this evening. You go ahead and dance with Tori, and we'll catch up with you later. Come, Tucker."

Her husband nodded and helped her to her feet before guiding her toward the town attorney.

Tori watched them for a few seconds while she gathered her nerve then smiled down at Garret as she held out her hand. "It sounds like we have our orders."

He searched her face just long enough she half expected him to refuse her or to follow his parents. But he nodded as he rose, setting down his napkin. Then he extended his elbow for her hand and led her to the dance floor. The official sets had just taken place: Trevor and Denae's first dance together. Denae's with her dad, Stewy, and Trevor's with his mom, Gloria. Then Trevor had done the honors with Denae's mother then her stepmom while Denae looked to be having way more fun with Russ Delgado.

Now it was a free-for-all. Kade danced with Cheri while, nearby, their daughter Harmony encouraged her littlest brother to twirl, but the one-year-old simply ran in circles, giggling. Several of the other kids were showing off their moves, and Jericho stomped his little cowboy boots with the best of them.

But then Tori and Garret stood along the fringes, and she turned toward him, clasping his left hand in her right as she slid her other hand up his bicep. Her skin tingled as his right hand touched her waist. For all he'd promised to be a poor partner, he knew his position. A guy with so much music in him would know more than that.

Garret began to swing to the tempo, leading Tori with him, but looking just past the side of her head. That's how Dad had taught her, as well, that looking at each other would shift their body positions and tangle their feet. For the first time, Tori had no desire to dance exactly correctly. She'd gladly take tangled feet if only she could gaze into Garret's eyes.

Right. In front of hundreds of people who knew them. She might not care, but Garret was much more withdrawn than she was. He wouldn't want the entire town speculating, but Tori had already started that in motion.

She inhaled the scent of him, just enough cologne to offset the hint of horse. She longed to finger the closely shaven angular jaw right at eye level. Good thing both her hands were busy, one resting on the black tux but feeling his muscles move as they danced, the other clasped firmly in his. Tori closed her eyes for a second, memorizing the points of contact, reveling in them.

When she opened them again, his gaze was fixed on her, his blue eyes searching hers for... something, but what? She offered him a tremulous smile. "You're not dancing like someone with two left feet."

"I can remedy that." And he said it with a straight face, too.

"I like this better."

His jaw twitched. "You can't have everything."

Tori felt her eyebrows hike. "And why not? Some people seem to have their destiny on a silver platter. A lot of our friends, actually."

"The world is full of tragedy. Just because a few people have found happiness doesn't mitigate that fact."

She squeezed his hand. "Mitigate is such a big word for a cowboy."

"Not all cowboys are dumb and uneducated."

Aha. There was the opening she'd been poking for. "Where did you go to school?"

"Back east."

She flicked his shoulder. "I kind of figured that part. Is it a big secret?" Then she held her breath.

"Why does it matter to you, Tori?"

"Because *you* do." Oh, great. Way to blurt that out.

Garret shook his head. "I'm not that interesting, honestly. Took some music school. Decided to move west. End of story."

"Wow, you make Reader's Digest condensed seem as detailed as *War and Peace*."

He pulled his gaze away from hers, his fingers flexing against her waist. "None of it is pertinent anymore."

"Garret?"

He glanced at her. Moisture glistened above his lip and shone on his forehead. "What?"

"What happened back there that you wish you could forget?"

"If something happened back then that I wished to forget, why would I want to talk about it?"

Fair point. Should she back down or keep pushing? It was so hard to know, especially since he didn't seem predisposed to sharing with anyone at all, not just her.

The song ended and a new one began. Or, rather, a golden oldie. Dolly Parton and Kenny Rogers belted out *Islands in the Stream*. "You hear that?" Tori asked. "People need each other. We aren't meant to be solitary."

"Big word for a cowgirl."

She waggled her eyebrows. "There's more where that came from. I was once planning to become a teacher."

"I can see you suited for that." Was that relief ebbing from his eyes? Of course. She'd turned the attention away from him. "Why didn't you?"

"Everything changed with Dad's accident."

Garret's forehead furrowed. "But... wasn't that a long time ago?"

"Ten years." At his lack of understanding, she sighed. "I was still in high school. James left college to take care of the ranch. Meg went crazy."

"So someone had to be the good daughter."

"I guess. There was a lot to do, transitioning a cattle ranch into a resort. It took all the finances we could muster there for a while. All the time, energy, creative thinking. A lot of risk."

"Right. But it's doing pretty well now, isn't it?" He shook his head quickly. "Don't answer. It's none of my business."

Ha, because if he got to probe, so did she? "It's fine. Yes, we're operating in the black."

"Do you still want to be a teacher?"

"It crosses my mind occasionally." But not when she danced with Garret. At the moment, all she wanted was to sail away with him to another world like in the song that was just ending. She'd rather be a wife — Garret's wife — and the mother of his children than pour her passion into other people's kids.

He shrugged, and her hand rose and fell with his shoulder. "Then do it."

"Just that easy?"

They stopped swaying as the music faded. Garret's hands released her. "Why not?"

Tori took one step closer and fingered both his lapels. The fragrance of the daisy on his boutonniere engulfed her as she brushed it. "Because I'm hoping there's more to life. I have other dreams, too."

Garret backed up, right into someone passing behind him. He tore his gaze from Tori, muttered an apology, and pivoted away.

Had the apology been for the wedding guest or for her? And what did it matter? She'd all but presented her heart to him, and he'd rejected her.

Guess her answer was clear.

And the entire town had witnessed it.

GARRET SKIRTED the dance floor in search of his parents. There they were, sitting at one of the round tables near the kitchen pass-through, visiting with the Berkleys. He shook Fred's hand then Irene's before pulling out a chair.

"Enjoying the wedding?" asked the attorney's wife. "Looked like you were having a nice dance with Tori Carmichael."

No doubt the entire community of Saddle Springs was going to speculate for a while. Great. "She was telling me her dreams of being a teacher."

"Sometimes young people have to leave for an education to come back." Fred nodded. "It was that way for me. I grew up here but attended the School of Law in Missoula. Met my lovely wife there." He patted her hand.

Garret's boomerang had been even more dramatic. He'd left home for college, too, though he hadn't gone far. But when he'd ricocheted back to the nest, they'd moved that nest clear across the country for a brand new start.

What would he do when his parents passed on? Was Saddle Springs truly his home now, or would he return to Kentucky? Or just keep moving on. Alone.

Tori offered something more, but she didn't really know him. Didn't realize that everyone he loved deserted him, one way or another. He was pushing her away for her own good. If he explained it all, he'd be letting her too close. He'd be in danger of losing his heart again, and that couldn't happen.

No, he'd started as he needed to continue.

The evening's master of ceremonies, Denae's Uncle Ted, invited everyone closer as the newlyweds cut their cake. Garret settled back in his seat. He didn't need a close-up of Denae mashing frosting into Trevor's face, or any view at all. A cheer went up and cameras seemed to flash forever.

At his mother's concerned look, Garret left their table and found the local veterinarian, Wyatt Torrington. The middle-aged man was always willing to talk about his experiences. They fell into an easy conversation as Wyatt regaled him with tales of horses he'd worked with over the years. When Wyatt moved on, Garret offered to sit with Howard Haviland so Spencer and Carmen could dance. The aging rancher seemed bright tonight, his eyes shining with all that went on around him.

Carmen's little daughter, Juliana, leaned on Garret's arm. "Dance with me?"

He smiled at the child's winsome face. "I don't want to leave your Uncle Howard alone."

She pressed her hands on either side of the old man's leathery face. "You don't mind, do you, Uncle Howard?"

He patted her blond hair. "You go on, missy. Have fun."

Juliana tugged at Garret's hand. "Come on then!"

Garret couldn't resist the child. He'd regret it, for sure, but he couldn't think of another way to extricate himself. Only, how did one dance with a girl who barely came past his waist?

"I want to twirl," Juliana informed him.

So it was easy. He held her hand, and she twirled until he felt as wobbly as she must. In between, he took a step right or left, and she followed his lead.

"Oh, dance with me!" Harmony Delgado pulled on Garret's arm. "That looks fun."

"We can take turns," agreed Juliana, stepping aside and nearly tumbling from dizziness.

What had Garret gotten himself into?

"It's time for the bride to toss her bouquet!" announced Ted Essery. "If all the single women would please come over here."

Wait. How had Garret managed to get close to the mic stand? "Come on, girls." He pulled at both hands. "Let's get out of the way."

"I want to see," insisted Harmony. "This is the fun part. At Mommy and Daddy's wedding, Auntie Lauren caught it and then she was married. I want to see who gets married next."

Garret did not. "Okay, you stay. I'm going to get a glass of punch." He managed to disengage the little girls' hands then edged through the oncoming women toward the drinks. Tori flashed him a smile on the way by.

Oh, no. There wasn't anything to this silly ritual, was there? Because she looked like she was going to leap in the air and fight for those flowers with everything she had.

A flush crept up Garret's neck, and he focused on pouring a glass of punch, his back to the happenings.

"Ready, set, go!" called Denae's uncle.

Okay, Garret couldn't resist after all. He turned just in time to see Tori capture the mass of pink roses and white daisies as it shot straight at her chest. Beside her, Anna made a moue of disappointment as cheers went up.

Tori turned to look at Garret. Their gazes caught and, for just a second, there was no one else in the community center banquet hall.

Then he shook his head and broke the contact.

Garret gulped the punch, set the glass down, and headed for his parents. On second thought, there was no way to get them out of the room in time. He swerved toward the double doors propped open to the June evening and headed straight through them, down the steps, through the parking lot, and to the riverside beyond.

If someone came looking for him for the ridiculous garter toss, they'd never find him. He'd make sure of that.

Oh, Jenna. Why did you leave me?

But the desperation in his thoughts was not as deep as it had been the first few years. His life would have been completely different had she lived. He wouldn't have even become the same man. The horrific accident that had claimed his bride had changed him forever. It had turned him into the man who'd been too blind to see through Chantelle Devereaux. Had turned him into the man who'd fled west like a kid who still depended on his parents.

It had turned him into the person he was today, a man who shielded his heart above everything else, even when it desperately wanted to love again.

He wanted to love Tori Carmichael.

He didn't have the courage.

CHAPTER 9

I 'm sorry." Lauren took a seat at the little kitchen table in Tori's cabin. She'd given James a kiss and told him she'd be home soon.

Standing at her kitchen counter, Tori wasn't sure whether to be thankful or annoyed with her sister-in-law. She unwound the ribbon holding Denae's gorgeous bouquet together so she could put the flowers in water. "I'll be fine." She managed to keep her voice even.

"Such a bummer, though. You guys danced for two entire songs. I thought he was coming around, but then...."

Tori shrugged, not looking at Lauren as she snipped the stems of the pink roses. She blinked back tears pricking the corners of her eyes. It wouldn't take much to snap and start bawling like a baby.

"Tori? Talk to me."

She took a deep breath. "It was a beautiful wedding. Everything went off without a hitch. I guess all Denae's planning paid off."

"Victoria June. You're as bad as Garret."

"What exactly is that supposed to mean?"

"I realized the other day that for as long as he's lived in Saddle Springs and how affable he comes across, he doesn't open up to anyone. I asked James about it, and he said the same."

Tori managed a chuckle. "Now that's the pot calling the kettle black. Because my brother doesn't, either."

"He does, though. He and Kade have been close since they were little cowpokes together."

Well, of course. It was just his sisters he kept out of his confidence. Meg might not have noticed half the time, but Tori had. All she wanted was to bond with her siblings. Be real friends. Good luck with that.

Lauren's voice softened. "I know you want to be closer to him, but my point is that there was someone he could confide in. Someone who knew him deeply and well, whereas Garret opens up to no one. Maybe to his parents, but I kind of doubt that."

"Maybe he has a close friend back east he talks to."

"Wouldn't we have heard of that person by now? It's not like Garret keeps to himself all the time. I mean, James knows him as well as anyone, I think. They've been leading worship together for over four years. They meet together weekly. Pray together. James didn't realize until I asked him just how close-mouthed Garret has been all this time. He's shared so little of his past."

Uh huh. Welcome to Tori's world.

"Maybe he's hiding something big."

Tori glanced over at Lauren. "Or blocking it." As the words came out, she recognized the likelihood of that. "I have no idea what, but it really seems he's protecting himself from something he refuses to deal with."

"You might have hit the nail on the head." Lauren tapped her chin as she stared out the patio doors to the lake beyond, lit only by a half moon.

"So, what if he never decides to move forward?" She stabbed a rose into the vase.

Lauren's gaze swung to meet Tori's.

Uh oh. She'd voiced her fear out loud. Might as well dump the whole thing. "I've been so stupid. I like him. I do. He's a nice guy who treats his parents well. He works hard. He loves the Lord and uses his musical talents in the church. There's nothing not to like."

Lauren nodded. "And how he danced with Juliana and Harmony tonight. Too cute."

"I know, right? He... he'd be a great dad." Tori swallowed hard, tucking a spray of baby's breath between two rosebuds. "I'm not a kid, but I've been acting like a teen with a crush on the popular boy."

"I doubt Garret was ever the star quarterback or the guy every girl swooned over. He's too unassuming."

Tori gave up on the partially arranged bouquet and leaned against the counter, crossing her arms. "Maybe. Or maybe something happened that changed him. The point is, he really hasn't given me any reason to pin my romantic dreams on him. Yeah, every once in a while he looks at me with *something* in his eyes, but maybe it's just a warning that he sees how blatant I am and wishes I would stop already."

"I don't think—"

She sliced her hand to cut off her sister-in-law's

words. "Five years, Lauren. Five years I've watched him, admired him, dreamed about him. I'm twenty-seven years old. How pathetic is that? He clearly doesn't feel the same. How long do I put my life on hold for something that won't ever happen?"

"I doubt..."

"Seriously? Do you know anything I don't? Has he said anything to James? Don't hold back if he has."

Lauren shook her head. "I'm pretty sure he hasn't."

Tori's heart fell. "That's my answer then. I gave it my best shot." She fingered her short, auburn-tinted hair. "If he noticed my haircut or my new clothes, he never said a word."

"I wondered if Garret was behind your trans-formation."

"Denae thought it might help."

Lauren's mouth twisted a little. "You went to Denae for help?"

Tori heard the unspoken words: *and not me?* "It's not like that. You know what a romantic she is. She sees love under every rock. It was all her observations and ideas."

"I guess I can see that. So, Garret left you in the middle of the dance floor. Do you want James to talk to him? Corner him?"

"No way." Just the thought made Tori squirm in embarrassment. "Too many people already saw me stitch my heart to my sleeve and parade it around. No. I have to set this whole thing aside. Focus on something else."

Lauren's eyes widened. "Some other guy? Not Sawyer, I hope."

"Never Sawyer. Didn't you see him sneak out early

with Anna? And besides, I've never been able to stand him. The guy has some serious growing up to do before he'll be fit for anything or anyone. I don't know what Anna is thinking."

"True that." Lauren snapped her fingers. "You used to want to be a teacher, and you're so good with kids. I see you all the time with the resort's young guests. Why not...?"

"I don't know. I wouldn't be able to get in until January at the earliest, since admissions for September closed a long time ago. And do I really want to go to college with kids ten years younger than me?"

"Why not? You've got maturity on your side. You'd do well, I know, and have more job offers than you'd know what to do with after graduation." She grimaced. "Not that I want you to leave Saddle Springs. I like having a sister nearby, and it seems I've only just started to get to know you."

That beat Meg's response. "I don't know," Tori said again. "I don't have to decide about college for a couple of more months, but I'm not sure I can wait until the new year to do something. Now that I've decided to end the stupid waiting game, I don't know how I can sit around and do the same old thing every day."

"The resort is busy. The summer will go quickly. Besides, I'm not sure what your parents would do without you leading the trail rides and all."

"I'd hate to leave them in the lurch. That's true. But I think they'd understand. There are teens in town who'd be happy for summer work. Matt was asking about a job for a friend just a couple of days ago." Tori thought about that for a minute. "Anyway, nothing will likely come of it. I just feel so... stuck. Like a hamster on a wheel. You know?"

"Everything changed for all of you with your father's accident." Sympathy lined Lauren's face.

"Well, yeah. And I'm still sorry it happened, but mostly for Dad's sake. I'd say in a lot of other ways it turned out for the best, even though James couldn't finish college."

"He's pursuing his degree online."

"Oh, that's great!" Another example of how little Tori knew about anything. "And Mom is so outgoing and hospitable that transitioning to a guest ranch has really made her thrive. It's been a good change."

"For everyone but you."

"And it's not all about me." Not for her parents. Not for Garret. Not for anyone.

Her sister-in-law's phone buzzed, and she glanced at it. "It's James, wondering when I'm coming."

At least Lauren had someone who noticed and cared when she wasn't around. "Go on home. Thanks for caring."

Lauren gave her a swift hug. "You sure you're okay? I'll keep praying for you. God will show you what He's got for you. I know it."

"Thanks. I appreciate it." She really, really did.

GARRET SQUIRMED in his seat the next morning in church. He'd have skipped if he hadn't been leading worship. Not only did he not want to face anyone — Tori, especially — but his parents seemed more exhausted than expected. They hadn't wanted to miss a minute of the lengthy wedding reception, but it had been too much. Mom hadn't even been out of bed this morning when Garret left for soundcheck. Unheard of. Them missing church was even more unheard of. *Not neglecting to meet together, as is the habit of some, but encouraging one another*, and all that. Hebrews 10:25. One of the hundreds of scriptures Dad had drilled into him over the years.

And then Garret'd had to face the songs he and James had chosen to go with Pastor Roland's sermon on Jesus' words to the disciples in the midst of the storm, "Take courage." Like Garret knew anything about that topic. He'd pivoted on his heel on the dance floor and left Tori standing alone in a celebratory crowd. The act of a coward, not a man of valor.

Her devastated expression as he turned away would be etched in his memory forever, right up there with Jenna's lifeless blood-covered face and Chantelle's smug defiance as she walked away with his sheets of hand-scribbled music and the career he'd had all but in his grasp.

This time he'd been the one to do the walking. This time he'd guarded himself from falling in love. It was a trap, anyway. Maybe not for every guy, but it was for him.

Except the walls he'd built weren't thick enough to keep every feeling out. He felt, all right. He felt like a heel. He felt like his heart was broken all over again. That he hadn't fallen in love with Tori was a lie he'd been telling himself for at least two years.

Courage. What a laugh.

"We are to be unsinkable saints in the storms of life."

Garret's attention had wandered, but those words of Pastor Roland's caught him and tugged him back.

"I don't need to tell anyone here that storms will come." The pastor paused and leaned on the podium. "Am I right? We have health storms. We have financial storms. We have relationship storms. Hiding in a corner with an umbrella above our heads may lull us into thinking we're protected for a short time. But the storms will come, and some of them are inside us."

Garret closed his eyes, doing his best to keep his face as blank as it could be considering the turmoil inside. One of those squalls swirled within him, threatening to drown him or, at the very least, push him into an unwanted port.

"Storms are good for us. Without them, we will not grow. We will not be strong. We will be like hothouse flowers, not fit for serving in God's kingdom. Did you notice Jesus sent the disciples out in that boat to cross the Sea of Galilee? Did you notice that the storm came, and He *waited* to rescue them?"

Garret blinked and focused on his Bible, open on his lap. There it was, in Matthew 14:24-25. It didn't seem fair. Didn't seem very nice of Jesus. Didn't he know the disciples would be terrified out there with the wind and waves pummeling their little boat? Sure, the guys were fisherman and accustomed to the elemental extremes, but this seemed to be a storm of epic proportions. Not your average tempest in a teapot.

God hadn't been in any hurry to help Garret out, either. Even as the thought crossed his mind, his conscience jabbed. The little boy who'd watched his mother die of a drug overdose? That child had found a forever home with Tuck and Nancy Morrison in a few short weeks. Many kids in the system were shuffled from foster home to foster home, but he'd lucked out. Not luck, though. God had met him in the storm and given him a port of refuge.

The fresh college graduate whose brand new wife had died before they reached their honeymoon hotel? That man had been devastated. Shattered. But he'd turned to Jesus in the midst of his pain and been comforted. Strengthened.

The aspiring musician who'd sought to bolster his career by the company he'd kept? Then, stupidly, he'd actually fallen for Chantelle Deveraux — thought they were building something real — only to be double-crossed. Served him right, probably. But God had been there to pick up the pieces. Tuck and Nancy had feigned boredom with his retirement from teaching at the university and bought a riding stable clear across the United States, giving Garret the opportunity to start over. They'd owned a thoroughbred breeding ranch in Tennessee, so it was mostly the location of their new venture that shocked their circle of friends.

Garret startled back to attention when he heard the worshipers around him speaking in unison. What was going on?

"I didn't hear you. What did Jesus tell the disciples in the midst of the storm?"

"Take courage!" chorused the congregation.

"Did He say, 'close your eyes and hope for the best'?"

"No! Take courage!"

"Did He say, 'you're right to panic; it's a terrible storm'?"

"No! Take courage!"

"Did He say, 'this storm is all your fault'?"

"No! Take courage!" With each exchange, the voices strengthened, became bolder.

"Did He say, 'this will teach you not to come out in a boat ever again'?"

"No! Take courage!"

Take courage? Garret took a deep, shuddering breath. How could he do that? He'd seen a lot of life's storms and never wanted to see another. But Pastor Roland was right in one thing at least. Jesus met the disciples *in* the storm.

CHAPTER 10

I didn't see you in church." Mom's gaze assessed her when Tori slid in the backdoor at lunch time.

Tori took a deep breath. "That's because I didn't go."

"Why not?"

Did other women in their late twenties get this kind of interrogation for their actions? Wasn't she old enough to make her own decisions? Oh, right. She still lived at home. "I didn't sleep well last night." That at least was completely true.

"I'm sorry. So you didn't wake up in time?"

That would be an easy out, but it wasn't true. To not wake up in time meant she'd slept at all, and that seemed incongruent with the fact she'd seen the numbers on her clock at least once per hour. "I took Coaldust for a ride."

How she'd needed the escape, and so had the gelding. It had been far too long since she'd ridden for the sheer pleasure of a horse between her knees. There had been so many trail rides paced for the least experienced guest. So few chances to canter and cross creeks and climb steep trails and stop to pick daisies and lie on her back in a meadow soaking up rays while Coaldust whiffled her hair.

Mom searched her face as Meg strolled into the kitchen and set two-year-old Sophia down. The little girl scampered through to the living room as Meg looked between Tori and their mother.

"Everything okay? Missed you in church."

Tori sighed. "Because I didn't go. Does that really require the Spanish Inquisition?"

"Sor*ree*. I didn't notice you being tortured or burned at the stake."

"Funny, Meg. Can we just let it go? Sometimes a girl needs to be alone with God out in creation instead of cooped up in a building, okay? It's not a billboard announcing I've lost my faith. What can I do to help with lunch, Mom?"

Even though Meg and Eli and James and Lauren lived nearby, life on the Flying Horseshoe was busy enough with everyone coming and going that their parents had decreed Sunday lunch to be for the family so everyone could gather and spend time together. Otherwise, with Lauren's long hours as a veterinarian and the resort guests and everything, they might not get the chance to stay connected.

Normally, Tori loved it. Loved seeing her nephew and niece. Loved dissecting Pastor Roland's sermon. Loved eating Mom's comfort food instead of the ranch chef's more gourmet style. Not that eating Ollie's meals was ever a hardship.

Today, though, she was restless. The time alone with

God while riding had definitely helped, but it hadn't erased the uneasiness in her spirit. The time with Garret at the wedding reception last night was like a magnet in her mind. The instant she wasn't forced to pay attention to something else, she snapped back to the moment where he'd mumbled something and pivoted away from her like he'd been an arrow shot from a bow.

Maybe she should have gone to church. Maybe that would have distracted her away from the replay, but Garret would have been there, and she just couldn't handle watching him and James lead worship. He definitely wouldn't have skipped out and left the pastor in the lurch like he'd done to her last night. He wouldn't have shown any hint that the situation last night affected him in any way... because it hadn't.

Sure, he'd bolted, but that had been distaste. She'd put her sentiments out there and he'd been too kind, too shy, to flat-out tell her he didn't have feelings for her and never would. Whatever she'd seen in his eyes those few times had not been connection. They'd been something else. She hadn't figured out what, yet, but he was only aware of her as the annoying younger sister of his best friend.

Well, then. She'd scrape together her bruised ego and... she had no idea what. Something, though. Something valid that would get her out of Saddle Springs where she could regroup in peace.

"...get out the salad?"

Tori blinked at Mom's voice. "Sure." She turned for the fridge.

"What's going on?" asked Meg, quietly. "You seem unusually spacey."

"Thanks." It was impossible to keep the sarcasm out of her voice.

Meg pulled back. "What?"

Tori sighed. She'd longed to be closer to her big sister and, finally, Meg asked her a real question, and all she could do was snap? "Sorry." She pulled open the fridge and lifted out the big salad bowl.

Meg peeked under a lid on the counter to reveal a layered chocolate cake. "Yum, Mom. That smells awesome." She glanced back at Tori. "Wasn't that a gorgeous wedding?"

"Sure was." No denying it. "And Lisa managed not to snipe at Michelle. Win, win."

Meg laughed. "Well, Denae's mom and stepmom often goad each other, but they were both on their best behavior. Made it much nicer for Denae and Trevor. I wish we could have stayed longer, but Sophia tripped, hit the floor, and would not be consoled. She was so overtired."

Which meant her sister might not have witnessed Tori's humiliation, but someone would certainly tell her within the next twenty-four hours. It was surprising she hadn't heard about it at church from a 'concerned' congregant, like Lauren's mom, who lived to share juicy gossip. Or maybe Meg had heard, and that was why she brought up the wedding at all?

Too much second guessing. "You probably didn't miss much. More dancing. More food. The bouquet toss which Denae fired straight at me."

"Ooh. Gorgeous bouquet. Do you have a nice vase for the flowers? If not, I have one you can borrow."

Tori nodded. She'd nearly sent them home with Lauren. How could she stand to look at them and remember Garret's rejection?

"Who got the garter?"

"Sawyer." Tori rolled her eyes. "And you know better than to even start with that."

Meg laughed. "You've got that right, but I'm here to tell you that God has ways to pull a wanderer back to Him. Sawyer's not beyond redemption by any stretch."

Some had thought Meg too far gone a few years back, but God had wooed her back. "I sincerely hope and pray Sawyer comes back to the Lord, but that won't make him the right guy for me."

"Not when Garret Morrison is around."

From the corner of her eye, Tori saw Mom's eyebrows rise at Meg's dig. Best to squash this one right now. "There's nothing between us, trust me. We danced together a bit, but we're just friends." Or they had been. What they were now was anyone's guess.

"Okay." Meg dragged the word out as she studied Tori's face.

"I think we're ready to call everyone for lunch." Mom carried a bowl of sautéed vegetables toward the dining table. "Meg, can you grab the fried chicken from the oven? I'll get the potato salad."

Possibly the interrogation would resume, but Tori would do her best to divert attention. Good thing Meg's kids were so stinkin' adorable and kept the family's attention with their funny comments and over-all cuteness.

GARRET'S MOM cleared her throat. "There's something we need to tell you."

He paused, his fork loaded with steaming eggs halfway to his mouth. Garret didn't miss how his father's hand reached over and covered his mother's on the table. He had a sudden suspicion that he wasn't going to like this confession and lowered his fork to his plate. "Oh? What's that?"

They exchanged a tender look as Mom's fingers curled around Dad's.

Pain stabbed Garret's heart. He would never have entire unspoken conversations like this with the love of his life. But the pain wasn't just from longing for something he couldn't have. It was the sadness in both their eyes.

"I took your mother to the doctor on Friday."

"And?" Garret prompted, wary when they both remained silent.

"Her cancer's back, son."

"No." If only his vehement rejection were enough to banish the horror forever.

"We won't have a clear idea until they run more tests later this week. But it doesn't look good."

Cancer never looked good. "Why didn't you tell me?"

"You had a lot going on this weekend with the Delgado wedding," Mom said. "We didn't want to distract you."

And it would have, true enough. But still. "You didn't have to stay so late. If I'd known, I'd have brought you home early. I'd have—"

Mom squeezed his hand. "I know. But I want to enjoy the time I have left. I want the people I care about to know how much I love and appreciate them."

But her words caught in his mind. "The time you have left? Stay positive. They got rid of it last time, and they can do it again. I know it's a tough road, but you can do it." Man, did he know about the need for courage. He'd agonized along with them. Wished he could take the treatment for her. Protected her.

"We talked things over with the doctor, and I won't be having chemo."

"Of course, you will. You'll—"

"It's your mom's decision, Garret."

"How can you say that?" He shoved back, his chair tipping and clattering to the floor as he surged to his feet. "You can't just let it win. You have to fight."

She gave him a sad smile. "There comes a time when treatment can't really do anything, son. It may buy a little time, but it may not, and it made me so horribly sick two years ago. This is already more aggressive. I'm ready to meet my Savior."

Garret shook his head in denial. "So am I. That doesn't mean I'm eager to do so anytime soon." There'd been enough death in his life. His mother. Jenna. The demise of so many dreams and aspirations. Weren't humans designed to cling to life? They survived the most appalling devastation and came out stronger. Nancy Morrison could, too. She'd never been a quitter. He stared Dad hard in the eye. "How can you let her say this? Do this?"

Dad rose slowly to his feet.

When had his shoulders become hunched? When had the deeply etched lines arrived on his face? When had he gotten... old? Was it concern for his wife, or was there more? But one parent's health at a time was more than enough to deal with.

Dad straightened slightly and met Garret's gaze. He was once again the respected genetics professor and esteemed horse breeder of years gone by. "Your mother is my partner in life. She is not my possession. I can't *make* her do anything, nor do I wish to. She is her own person with her own thoughts, her own emotions, her own fears. Her own bravery. If you think she's made this decision lightly, flippantly, then you don't know the strong woman who raised you."

Swaying from the impact, Garret closed his eyes for a second. "I'm sorry, sir. Ma'am." He nodded at his mother. "I meant no disrespect." Everything in him screamed with defiance, though. "Excuse me, please. Noela will be here any minute to start her shift."

His mother nudged his plate. "You haven't finished your meal, dear."

Garret looked down. He'd eaten nearly half before they'd dropped the bombshell, and even that half sat like a hard lump in his belly. More food would not be an improvement. He pushed a smile toward his mom. "Sorry. My appetite seems to have fled."

"I'll be out to the stable after I help your mother clean up from breakfast."

Garret nodded. Most days, Dad persisted in ambling around the property as though he were actually doing something significant, but reorganizing the tack hadn't proved all that helpful. So they were alphabetical by horse now. Big whooped y-do. Garret had reached for the wrong halter more times in the past week than he could count because they weren't where they'd always been.

He pushed in his chair, scraped his plate into the garbage bin, and slotted it into the dishwasher. With a final nod, he grabbed his Stetson off the rack, tugged on his boots, and headed outside.

How could the grass shimmer from last night's rain while the morning sunshine angled above the eastern hills? How could the ranch smell fresh and sweet and the red-winged blackbirds trill in the cottonwoods along the creek? Didn't nature know that the Morrisons' lives were dark with doom?

He buried his face in Trudy's mane, arms wrapped around her neck. Even his chestnut mare wasn't immune to the passage of time. She was only eight, but he remembered her as the high-stepping filly she'd been when he bought her. It had been love at first sight.

Like with Jenna, but he refused to let his mind go there. Refused to remember her blond curls and her pixie face. Her habit of biting her lip when studying for her classes, the way her face lit up when she saw him, and the laughter that came so easily. He refused to remember her shining face as she came toward him swathed in white. And then… gone.

He could refuse all he wanted, but the memories were all there, jostling to erupt. He'd loved her with everything in him, but death had claimed her before he could.

Garret needed to ride, and the trapper's cabin called him. He'd spent so much time there when they'd first come west. It was a place that had salved his spirit in those desperate times. He strode into the tack room and grabbed Trudy's saddle and bridle.

"Going somewhere?" came Noela's voice from the alley as he swung the saddle to Trudy's back. "I thought we were exercising the horses on the other side today."

He could take Newton as easily as Trudy, but no. He needed his own horse. "Change of plans. Go ahead and start over there. I'll be back in an hour or two. Sorry."

"Garret?" Her voice was softer, closer. "Are you all right?"

Wasn't that the million-dollar question? "I will be." When he got to heaven himself someday, maybe. Not likely before then. He slid the girth strap through the loop and tightened it. With the saddle in place, he moved to Trudy's head with the bridle.

"I'll just get started then..."

"Thanks. My dad will be out shortly to lend a hand."

Noela gave a soft chuckle.

Yep, it didn't take any special insight to figure out Tuck Morrison was getting old, too.

Garret led Trudy out to the open yard, mounted up, and headed her toward his favorite vista trail. The pressure in his head and heart might explode without release, but old habits died hard. All he could do was pull everything a little closer to his chest and barricade against the pain as best he could.

CHAPTER 11

Dora Yanovich toyed with strands of Tori's hair and looked at her in the Shear Inspirations mirror. "I still think this style suits you."

Despite Sawyer's brief, sudden interest in her and Garret's second look then dismissal, Tori agreed. It took two minutes to blow-dry in the mornings and looked good all day, even when she was cleaning cabins between guests or trotting Coaldust on a mountain trail.

"So you're just wanting a trim then?" Dora peered at Tori's scalp. "I don't think the roots need touching up. Maybe next time, but the mahogany is so close to your original color that it blends in well."

"Yes, just a trim. Thanks."

Dora whipped a cape around Tori's shoulders, snapped it up, and spritzed her hair. "So, did you catch your young man?"

Tori nearly choked on the oxygen that had been flowing freely an instant before. She'd nearly forgotten how snoopy her sister-in-law's mother could be. "Pardon me?"

"Oh, you know." Dora waved her scissors slightly, and Tori managed not to flinch. "You've had your eye on that Morrison fella for a while now."

"I had my hair done because Denae suggested something fresher for her wedding." Tori put as much authority in her voice as she could muster.

"Oh, come on. I saw how you two danced together before he went storming off. Have you made up? It's been weeks now."

"I simply told him something he didn't wish to hear. There was no romance before or after." In her dreams, perhaps, but she wasn't telling Lauren's mom that, because she'd likely tell the next person to sit in her chair and, before another day went by, half of Saddle Springs would be in the know.

Snip, snip. "Well, that's too bad. Neither of you is getting any younger."

Time for a diversion. "Are you still seeing Doc Torrington?" Lauren had been shocked to find her veterinarian partner embracing her mother a couple of years back. The two had dated for a while, but Tori didn't remember seeing them together at the wedding.

Dora narrowed her gaze at Tori in the mirror. "How are things at the Flying Horseshoe? All booked up, I hope?"

She'd take the topic change, thanks. Nice to know there was a way to keep the town gossip from probing. "Yes, it's a busy summer. We've got a full house for the next two weeks with a girls' school from Boston coming in."

"A school? Aren't they on break in July?"

"Apparently they offer some trips and getaways through the off-season as well."

"Well, isn't that interesting?" Dora's flat voice proved she didn't think so. For a few minutes, she focused on Tori's hair.

With each snip, Tori's mind drifted further. Was the entire town speculating about Garret walking away without bothering to escort her off the dance floor, or was it just Dora? Had anyone besides Tori noticed that Garret had all but disappeared since the wedding? She'd only seen him at a distance.

It was like he lived in his own world. He slipped out of church via the side door right after the benediction and skipped Thursday night gatherings at The Branding Iron. All because she'd dared to dance with him and tell him she felt something for him.

Sheesh, cowboy. Just tell her there was no hope. She didn't need all this drama. Not when she was already feeling all the pressure of doing something useful with her life, since marriage and kids didn't seem to be in her future.

Dora massaged product into Tori's hair then grabbed the blow-dryer and aimed it at her head. A minute later she stood behind Tori, fluffing her hair. "There you go, hon. Looks good, don't you think?" She angled a hand mirror for Tori to inspect the back.

"Thanks, Dora. It feels lighter and more manageable again."

The chair settled to the floor and the stylist swiveled it away from the mirror. "Excellent. Do you want to book your next appointment while you're here?"

"Um, sure. I can do that." Tori pulled her wallet out of her purse and followed Dora to the counter.

The salon door pushed open, and an elderly woman entered.

Tori sucked in a breath. Garret's mom. When had she shrunk so much? "Hi, Mrs. Morrison."

"Why, hello, dear." Her smile was warm even though her face seemed sallow. "That hairstyle looks lovely on you. Dora does an excellent job."

At the compliment, Tori patted the side of her head. "Thank you. And, yes, I agree."

"Go ahead and have a seat in my chair, Nancy." Dora held the magnetic strip card reader out to Tori. "I'll be with you in two shakes of a lamb's tail."

But Nancy Morrison's hand rested on Tori's arm. Her hand with blue veins clearly defined beneath mottled skin. "Are you in town for a bit longer? I'd love to have coffee with you at Java Springs when I'm done here."

From the corner of her eye, Tori caught Dora looking eagerly between them. Great. "I'm sorry, Mrs. Morrison. I'm expected back at the Flying Horseshoe to lead a trail ride in—" she made a show of checking her watch "—twenty minutes. Maybe another time?"

Nancy squeezed gently. "Another time, then."

Dora handed the receipt across the counter, and Tori took it and fled. What had that all been about? Did Nancy want to tell her to stop badgering Garret? Probably. He was the child of their old age, so she likely felt protective. Nancy must have been over forty when she gave birth to him. Closer to fifty? To what age were women fertile, anyway? Tori didn't even know, but Mrs. Morrison must have been pushing the limits.

The July day promised to be a scorcher. Tori tugged her sunglasses from her purse and slid them into place then caught sight of Tuck Morrison's gray truck with the Canyon Crossing Stables emblem on the door. Garret's dad sat in the driver's seat and lifted a hand to greet her when their gazes connected.

Tori waved back and hurried away. She was dying of curiosity as to what Garret's mom wanted to talk about, but the fear of finding herself in a frank discussion about her emotions and Garret's lack of them was completely unappealing.

No, she'd do without that little talk if at all possible.

"WHAT SONGS DO we know that reflect the forgiveness of sins?" James tapped a pen on his spiral-bound notebook as he sat in Garret's music room.

"Chris Tomlin's *Amazing Grace*," suggested Lauren.

She didn't join them often, but was here today, helping plan the next Sunday's song list for worship.

Garret's fingers found the keys and began to play.

"I like that." James nodded. "Broken chains. Being set free. Mercy like a flood... all those are present in the story in Mark 2 that Pastor Roland is preaching from."

"There's a lot of faith in the story, too." Lauren ran her finger down her phone app, eyes scanning the lines. "Think of how much faith those four guys had, ripping apart a roof and lowering their friend through it." She looked up. "They knew all they had to do was get their friend in front of Jesus."

"Right, but the pastor is focusing on Jesus' words through the gospels." James leaned over his wife's shoulder and pointed. "So the point is in verse five, 'Son, your sins are forgiven.'"

Garret tuned them out as he played through *Amazing Grace* again, adding embellishments and listening to the lyrics in his head. The contemporary chorus riffed off John Newton's classic.

Those chains the song spoke of. They were definitely weaker than they had been, but were they fully dissolved? If not, was it because Garret was weak in faith?

The guy in the Bible story, though. It was his friends' faith that got him to Jesus and totally healed, inside and out. The dude was paralyzed, for goodness' sake. It wasn't like he could transport himself there.

Garret glanced over to see James's and Lauren's heads bent over her Bible app together, their dark hair blending together. His friends couldn't help bring him to Jesus. They thought he was already there.

A tap on the music room door sounded then Garret's dad poked his head in. "I'll just set the mail on the table here, and you can get to it when you have a minute. There's some bills and, uh..." The expression on his face seemed guarded. "Something else you'll want to see, I believe."

What on earth? Garret turned from the piano and picked up the stack of envelopes. A sheet of paper fluttered to the floor. It had been folded and then pressed open, probably by Dad.

And a familiar face smiled innocently up at him.

His first reaction was to stomp on it, but Lauren's voice stopped him. "Oh! We got one of those flyers in the mail, too. That's Chantelle Devereaux, isn't it?" Lauren picked up the paper and held it out to him. "She's got an amazing voice, and man, can she play piano! Nearly as good as you, Garret. Have you heard of her?"

Had he *heard* of her? Garret stared at the black-and-white photograph. "I've heard of her."

"She's doing a concert in Spokane in a few weeks. See the dates? I wish she'd come to Missoula, but I'm sure we're way too small for someone like her."

So had he been. Much too small, too insignificant. Not when she could use him to boost her to the bottom rung of the ladder of success. Looked like she'd figured out how to climb the rest of the way on her own... unless she'd found other guys to use along the way. Which was likely.

"We should get a carload or two together and drive over for her concert." James took the flyer from Lauren's hand. "It's a Friday night. We could stay in a hotel or come back late."

"I don't think so." Garret didn't even recognize his voice with the harsh undertone. "I'm not interested."

Lauren angled her head up at him. "Really? I'm surprised. I would have thought her music would be right up your alley."

Her music was so up his alley it was like he might have written it. Oh, wait. He had. He managed to hold the bitter laugh in. "We should get back to the song list for Sunday. So *Amazing Grace* is in. What else?" He turned and sat down at the piano. His hands awkwardly hit the keys, resulting in a discordant sound. "Sorry."

"If I didn't know better, I'd think you actually knew this person." Lauren snatched the paper from James and held it toward him. "And didn't like her. A long-lost sweetheart, perhaps."

Garret took a deep breath and forced himself to meet her gaze. "Give it up, Lauren. Can we get back on track? I have a horse in the stable that seemed to be limping earlier. I need to check her out soon."

"Which one? I'll have a look."

He'd forgotten for a sec that he was talking to a veterinarian. "She'll probably be okay." In fact, the limp was so minute it likely didn't exist. "Other songs?"

"How about *Forgiveness* by Matthew West?"

Lyrics slammed Garret's mind. Forgiveness for people who didn't deserve it. Loving. Reaching out. Doing the impossible.

Had he ever forgiven Chantelle?

Nope. And today wasn't going to be the day, either. "I don't think that one's as easy for congregational singing. Any other ideas?"

He didn't miss the look Lauren and James exchanged, but there was no way he was going to elaborate. When he could force memories of Chantelle out of his mind, he could convince himself that he was a growing believer, secure in his faith and love for his Lord. But when she pushed her way in, he knew. It was all an act. An adhesive bandage attempting to cover a festering wound.

He was not healed.

CHAPTER 12

T hirty preteen girls and six chaperones filled the cabins at the Flying Horseshoe. They'd shown up in matching black T-shirts no less, each back emblazoned with the logo of their elite school. All the better to keep track of kids in airports, Tori guessed. At least now they wore regular clothes. Maybe now she'd be able to start seeing personalities and telling them apart.

Eager faces looked from her to the horses and back again, but several stood in the back, arms crossed, wearing boredom like masks. There were some in every crowd. One little girl with blond ringlets cast furtive smiles toward James, who didn't seem to notice. There was one of those in every group, too.

"Okay, fifteen of you and two of your leaders will come on a trail ride now. The others will stay here at the lake." Tori pointed toward the small body of water. "Whoever wants to paddle a kayak may, or if you want to swim, that's fine, too. There are other floaties, like that giant unicorn. Four of your leaders will be here for you, and my sister, Meg, will help the kayakers. My brother, James, and I will lead the trail ride." She beckoned Ms. Johnson, the group leader, over. "If you'll announce the first riders, please?"

The tall, thin woman nodded briskly and strode closer. She consulted her clipboard and began to read off the names. The girls moved to one side as their names were called. The blond who crushed on James clapped her hands and giggled as she joined her friends.

Seriously? She couldn't be more than ten. Tori had not been that kind of kid. At ten, it had all been about horses, not boys, and especially not men three times her age. She shook her head.

The other leaders rounded up the remaining girls and headed to the cottages for swimsuits while Tori and her siblings began hoisting girls onto waiting horses.

"I'm Lillian," the ringletted girl announced to James as he helped her onto Snowball.

Tori paused to watch.

"I'm James. My wife and I live here at the ranch. Where are you from?"

Tori stifled a chuckle as the child's face saddened. And here she'd thought her brother hadn't noticed.

"Medford," mumbled Lillian, looking away. She gathered the reins.

"Have you ridden before?"

She nodded. "My daddy has horses."

"All right then. Stay put until everyone is mounted up."

James shifted to the next kid, and so did Tori. Soon she swung up onto Coaldust and let her brother lead the group out while Matt and Lionel, the teen employees, headed back to the stables to clean vacant stalls.

The girls fell into line behind James with their two chaperones interspersed among them. Lillian hung back, and Tori gave her a smile. "Off you go, and I'll be right behind you."

The girl sighed and nudged Snowball into motion. She glanced over her shoulder as though to ensure there was a rearguard. They filed around the north edge of the lake then James angled up one of the trails to the upper meadows, an easier route for inexperienced riders. Soon the path widened, allowing the riders to break out of their single line.

Lillian looked at Tori as she reined in alongside. "This is a nice horse. Is she for sale?"

Tori smiled and shook her head. "Snowball? No. She's lived on the Flying Horseshoe since she was a foal, and her daughter was born here."

"A baby horse?" Lillian's blue eyes shone. "Can I see her?"

Tori chuckled. "Rosebud's not little anymore. She's two years old, and we're training her for riders." She leaned toward the girl. "But Snowball is going to have another foal in springtime."

"Really?" Lillian reached down and ran a hand along the mare's side. "There's a baby in there?"

"There is. A horse is pregnant for most of a year, but Snowball is fine being ridden this summer. She likes getting into the mountains."

"I like it, too." The girl sounded wistful. "We don't have mountains in Boston."

"No, I guess you don't." Saddle Springs might chafe at Tori these days, but she couldn't imagine living in a big eastern city. Some of the chaperones taught at the all girls' school. They probably made pretty good money, but that wouldn't be enough to lure Tori away from Montana's ranching country.

The battle raged inside her. Leave everything she knew behind and get her teaching degree? Or stagnate as an old maid, working for her parents until they died and she became part owner of the Flying Horseshoe by default? No kids of her own, just the maiden aunt to Sophia and Aiden and any kids James and Lauren ever had. She'd get the house, since her sister and brother had their own newer builds around the end of the lake.

That future stretched in front of her in chilly, dismal gray, contrasting sharply to the warmth and beauty in the high meadow today. Brilliant orange Indian Paintbrushes beamed amid yellow balsamroot, deep purple gentians, and dainty white woodland stars. Pinky-purple fireweed climbed the steep slope across the meadow where a mudslide had taken out a strip of forest a few years back.

Bumblebees danced among the flowers, not audible amid the creaking leather, grunting horses, and chattering girls.

Tension oozed out of Tori as she took off her hat and tilted her face toward the sun, allowing the sweet fragrance of the meadow drift into her awareness. Somehow, she had to keep this, no matter what happened. No matter that Garret didn't love her. No matter that no one besides her family did.

Around her, the girls dismounted, intent on picking

bouquets to decorate their cabins. Lillian slid off Snowball and joined them.

Only then did James sidle closer on Jigsaw and pull up beside Tori. "Wow, that one is quite the kid."

Tori chuckled. "Lillian? Yeah. Poor little city girl in love with a big, brusque cowboy."

He rolled his eyes. "In love? That's what you call a kiddie crush these days?"

"Let her down gently." She wished Garret had done the same instead of abandoning her on the dance floor.

"I think I did." James studied her as he lifted his hat to scrub a hand through his hair. "You doing okay?"

"Did Lauren put you up to this conversation? Because I don't think you've ever asked me that in my entire life."

He laughed. "Maybe. But it's a good question. You seem kind of quiet lately."

Tori shrugged. "I'll be fine. Just struggling a bit on what to do with the rest of my life. Is this my calling, herding rich people's kids around and trying to make sure no one gets hurt?"

"I get that." James scanned the group in the meadow. "I was restless, too, before things were settled with Lauren. Sometimes I felt trapped. I couldn't let Mom and Dad down, but I couldn't face Saddle Springs, either."

Her eyebrows hiked. Of course. Her brother was so much more introverted than she was, and even more tied to the ranch since he was the only son. "But then Lauren."

He gave her a sidelong look. "I was two years older than you *before Lauren*."

"Only because you were too fixated on waiting

because of your silly teenage promise instead of sweeping her off her feet years earlier."

"Yeah. Kind of." He combed his fingers through Jigsaw's blond mane, and the pinto shivered in delight. "But I didn't recognize that at the time. I just knew the decades stretched ahead of me with little to look forward to."

Tori swiveled in her saddle and stared hard at him. He did know. He did get it. "Yeah. Kind of where I'm at. Except I'm done deluding myself that there might be a change if I just keep waiting."

"You don't know that."

"So you're saying to just sit tight and wait? Wait for what, James? A miracle?"

"They happen every day." He grinned.

"Not to me." She narrowed her gaze as his grin stayed glued beneath bright eyes. "What's going on?"

"Just wanted you to know you're going to be an aunt again."

"You're telling me Lauren is pregnant?"

He nodded, and she leaned over and slugged his arm. "Congratulations. I think."

She wanted to be excited for them, but it was hard when she wanted the same thing for herself so badly.

"Thanks. Lauren's puking a lot. She might hate me round about now."

"Then she'll hate you more when she's actually giving birth."

He let out something between a laugh and a huff. "Probably."

"When's the baby due?"

"Early February." He stared off for a minute.

Tori followed his gaze toward the group of girls and their leaders clustered around a fallen log. All seemed well.

"Remember when Sophia was born?" he asked. "I was smitten when Meggie and Eli brought her home and I held her for the first time. I was so jealous of Eli. He had everything I wanted."

"Megan?" Tori kept her voice light.

James shot her a horrified look. "Not my sister, silly. But a wife. A baby. Just to be settled with a family, even though Eli says they didn't get a decent night's sleep for over a year."

A lot like she felt now. The longing was greater with her brother's words than it had been this morning, and it had nearly swamped her then.

James and Lauren had both waited for the other to make a move. Tori wasn't like either of them. She'd told Garret how she'd felt, and he'd walked away.

If there was to be another step in their dance, it was up to him. But there wouldn't be. He'd been clear.

GARRET CRASHED his hands onto the keyboard. Why would that new tune not leave him alone? It had been fine. He'd enjoyed working with the soulful measures until the lyrics had manifested themselves. Now he wanted a different melody. Anything else.

Hazel eyes with glints of green and brown and gold.
Gazing into the windows of your soul,

Everything you think is mirrored there—
I'm powerless against...

He'd felt even more powerless since he'd seen Chantelle's flyer. Oh, he'd never written an ode to her blue eyes, but he'd certainly lost himself in their shining depths.

He'd trusted her. Loved her. Convinced himself she loved him in return. That had been oh, so false.

Tori didn't love him, either. She was unlikely to stab him in the back like Chantelle had done, gutting his promising career, but Tori couldn't love him. She didn't know him.

Whose fault was that?

His. Everything was his fault. He was unable to open up and trust again. He wasn't made for long-term. Even Jenna would likely have found him wanting and left him at some point. Her death on their wedding night had taken the choice out of her hands, but Garret knew. He'd have messed up somehow, despite his best intentions, and she'd have given up.

Would she really? The rebuttal niggled him.

Sure, she would have, because Garret wasn't made to be loved. He was defective somehow.

He forced his hands back to the keys and played *Ten Thousand Reasons*. Forced Matt Redman's worshipful lyrics through his mind. Forced himself to bless the Lord.

No. He pushed away from the piano. He couldn't do it.

Not when his anger at Chantelle consumed him. His turmoil over Tori. His denial over his mom's cancer, which was every bit as invasive and advanced as his worst fears had been. He'd talked to the oncologist himself, but the man had patiently explained why treatment was not the right choice. It wasn't just Mom being deluded. See? Even she would leave him, probably in the next few months.

The pathway in his mind had become a deep rut he seemed unable to swerve out of. He could see it, but why fight it? It was based in truth.

He strode out of the music room and out the front door, blinking a little at the evening sun angling toward him, so opposite the storms inside.

Even God couldn't possibly love him like this. He'd embraced faith when his new mom had explained the Christmas story. He'd been a small child desperate to be accepted and loved, and Jesus sounded pretty cool. Not only did Jesus love him, his new mom did, too. It could only get better from here, right?

Wrong.

Yeah, he'd had a good childhood after the memories of his mother's lifeless body stopped waking him at night in a cold sweat. Nancy was an excellent pianist and offered lessons to neighborhood kids. Kellen, five years Garret's senior, had hated practicing. Garret had barely been able to wait for his brother to slide off the piano bench so he could climb up there and do it right.

Add Kellen to the long list of people who despised him.

Mom had let Kellen quit soon after and focused on teaching Garret, then got him a more advanced teacher when he outstripped her abilities in his early teens.

He'd really thought he was something back then.

The truth was much, much less. Just a thirty-year-old who could ride, write a little music, and play piano. Whatever. That was certainly no claim to fame.

Not like Chantelle Devereaux, who'd climbed the ladder on the backs of others... like him. No longer content with keyboarding for the band, now she was headlining.

He pulled the flyer from under a pile of paperwork on his desk in the stable's office and carried it out to the corral. Then, with fumbling hands, he lit the sheet. He watched the flame spread across the paper until it was consumed then stomped the remains into the dirt.

If only he could wipe away the traces in his heart.

CHAPTER 13

Y ou're so good with the girls."

"Thanks." Tori angled a glance toward Deb Gosselin, one of the chaperones for the girls' school, as the woman settled beside her on the sandy beach.

"Have you ever thought of becoming a teacher? The Lord only knows how much the world needs teachers who really love kids this age."

Really, God? Pray for guidance and get a stranger's encouragement? "The thought has crossed my mind a few times."

"Really?" Deb's face lit up. "Any school would be honored to have a teacher like you. I saw how gently you and your brother let Lillian down without crushing her and how patiently you've worked with all of them in teaching riding and plant identification and, well, everything."

The praise made Tori uncomfortable, but it also warmed her heart. "Just doing my job."

"More than that. We've taken the girls to a lot of

unique locations over the years I've worked at the school. Not everyone makes the effort you do at the Flying Horseshoe to partner with us in providing a nurturing and encouraging learning environment. We teachers have all spoken to Ms. Johnson about offering the guest ranch as an annual excursion."

Nearby, most of the girls played in the water, diving off the raft, kayaking, or trying to tip the giant inflatable flamingo. A few lay on the beach in swimsuits, slathered in tanning lotion. Tori remembered being their age, tipping back and forth from childhood to maturity like riding a playground teeter-totter.

"Thank you. We're honored. We'd need to work with you on dates for next summer soon, though, since your school needs every available cabin. We already have a number of bookings for next year."

"Good point, and I can see why you're booked so far in advance." Deb glanced toward the main house. "Whom do we see about starting that process?"

"Usually my sister Meg, but she's as busy as anyone this week with you all here."

"And she has such adorable children, too. What an idyllic place to raise a family."

Tori's heart squeezed at the thought of leaving the Flying Horseshoe or even Saddle Springs. "It's a great environment. So, you'd be best off catching my mom, Amanda. She can log into the database and put a hold on a week or two while your school admin determines if a return trip is what they'd like to do."

"I'll be sure to do that. Your mom is great. Everyone here is. It's been an exceptional few days." Deb jutted her chin toward the sunbathers. "Even the most hormonal have settled in."

Peyton and Aubrey had been the most disdainful of riding stinky smelly horses, but they'd come around. Tori stifled a chuckle. "On their own terms, but yes."

Deb leaned back, her arms braced in the sand. "You're really thinking of becoming a teacher? I can imagine how hard it would be to leave this place."

"That's the dilemma for sure." Tori cast her new friend a sidelong glance. "We all had to pitch in after my dad's accident, and I don't regret that." Much. "But maybe now..."

"I wondered what happened to him."

"A freak farming accident. He was cleaning out a piece of equipment when someone flipped on the auger absentmindedly. It caught his legs." Tori still shuddered at the very thought of how much worse it could have been.

Deb shook her head, eyes brimming with sympathy. "I can't imagine how hard that must have been. How much courage was required. You're a strong family."

"Our faith in Jesus is what kept us going. On our own, we're no stronger than anyone else."

"I've seen that faith in action this week. It's commendable."

Politeness nudged Tori to thank the teacher for those words, but it wasn't right. "It's not us. Trust me. It's all God. For every bit of honor we offer Him, He provides the peace and faith for the next round. It's like a cycle."

"Interesting." Deb watched the girls swim for a few minutes.

Was it really like a cycle? Offer faith, receive both

blessing and trial, which, when accepted, brought more faith to offer up? It sounded so simple.

It was anything but simple. They'd nearly lost Dad ten years back. Then they'd feared his legs would need to be amputated. Then came the realization he'd never walk again without help. That he was a rancher who couldn't ride. Couldn't drive a tractor. Couldn't clean a barn.

But they'd held onto each other and held the faith. Well, except for Meg, but she'd come back around. All those nightmarish experiences had taught their family the truth of Romans 8:28, that all things did work together for good, for those who loved God and were called according to His purpose.

They'd forged a new path for the Flying Horseshoe, one God had blessed. Through it, Tori could share her faith with guests like Deb, who'd taken the time to get to know her a little.

Could she do more as a teacher? Not in a public school, but maybe in a private one, if it were a Christian one. But then she'd be preaching to the choir, not reaching out to those who needed words of comfort and courage the most.

She could do that here.

But was it enough?

"PLEASE GIVE grace and peace through this difficult time, and we ask for Your will to be done. In Jesus' name, amen." Pastor Roland raised his head to smile at Mom, who lay on the sofa, covered with a fuzzy throw even in the July heat.

Garret craved finding comfort through prayer, but any glimpses he gained wafted from his grasp like so much steam from a hot cup of coffee. How had he managed to hold himself together after Jenna and then the mess with Chantelle, yet not now?

Because there was no one who had loved him longer, with a love more pure and sacrificial, than Nancy Morrison.

Except Jesus.

But that didn't count. Jesus was God. Of course, He'd come in first place.

"Is there anything I can do for you? Or the church?" The pastor looked from Mom to Dad then Garret. "Do you need meals?"

"No," blurted Garret. "We're fine. I can take her to appointments and cook." Which was a bit of a stretch, since he'd only managed not to burn the eggs twice yet. How could it be so hard?

"It's all right to accept help, you know," Pastor Roland said mildly.

Mom reached for Garret's hand. "You can't do everything, son. You've got the business to run. Doing the cooking and cleaning as well is too much."

It had been rather too long since the bathroom had been scrubbed and the kitchen counters completely cleared, but Garret wasn't ready to accept defeat.

He wasn't ready for the community — the church — to know how desperate their situation was. He wasn't ready for pitying looks or well-meant but stupid platitudes people said from the pinnacles of their perfect lives while others suffered.

Garret knew. This wasn't the first time he'd been the focus of others' prying eyes. It would come again. He knew he couldn't manage for much longer. But not yet. Not today.

"We're fine."

"If you're sure." The pastor turned to Dad. "Our people are always ready to step into the gap for families who need it. You only need to ask, and the church will send food and get some women in to clean. I know you don't drive much anymore, Tuck. We'll help with whatever you need. Give us the chance to serve you, as you have served us."

Dad glanced at Garret then back to the pastor. "Maybe next week."

The man sighed in disappointment but nodded.

Mom's eyes had already fluttered shut. She slept so much. Dad was caring for her, helping her to the bathroom, being within reach.

Was Garret being selfish? His heart cracked just a little. He probably was. Mom needed trained nursing care. Dad needed a break, though he wouldn't take it. Garret needed all kinds of help. Noela made the difference with the horses, but his office work was piling up, clients needed calling back, and the farrier was due to return next week.

And Garret was no kind of cook. A slight sniff was all that was required to catch the odor of burned eggs and something more sour that he couldn't get to the bottom of. It didn't take more than a quick glance to see dust on the side tables and cobwebs on the ceiling.

He closed his eyes and took a deep breath. All that stood in the way of getting the help his mom needed was his own pride... and his parents' understanding that he needed to come to grips with the situation on his own terms and in his own time.

Maybe that time was now. He rose to his feet and nodded to Pastor Roland. "May I see you out to your car?"

"Certainly." The man glanced at Mom, who slept with her lips slightly parted, her breathing shallow, then at Dad. He gripped Dad's hand. "Talk to you soon, Tucker."

Dad offered Garret a sad plea in his eyes, and Garret nodded.

They stepped out into the lingering heat of a July evening. Once again, Garret marveled that the planet seemed to go right on turning even though there was so much heartache.

"Friend, I wish you'd reconsider."

Accepting words tried to edge past the lump in Garret's throat, but they failed. He stared at the older man, tears stinging his eyes.

"For five years, you've led our congregation in worship nearly every week. Your passion for the Lord and the way you offer the talents He's given you have blessed every single member of our congregation. Please—"

"Yes."

Pastor Roland angled his head. "Pardon me? Did you say—"

"Yes." Garret scrubbed his hand through his hair. He'd forgotten his hat on the rack. That never happened. "It's my pride that's in the way, and that's selfish. Wrong. My parents don't deserve to suffer because I can't accept help."

The man's hand settled on his shoulder. "I get it. It's hard to let people in. But your mom—"

"She rescued me, Pastor. Her and Tuck. I was just a little kid, so needy." His voice caught. Choked.

"We all need our parents."

"You don't understand. I'd watched my mother d-die of a drug overdose. They adopted me."

"I didn't know."

"I can't bear to watch the mother of my heart die. I can't do it. Why is God asking it of me?"

"Oh, son." Pastor Roland's arm rounded Garret's shoulder and tugged him close for a few seconds. "If only there were easy answers. If only pastors had a sixty-seventh book of the Bible to pull out in times like this to recite verses that put everything into perspective. We don't. All we know is we live in a fallen world. We're beset with trials of every kind. Take courage. Jesus will walk with you through the storm."

Take courage. That had been the text for the sermon he'd first struggled with, back when his biggest problem was denying he loved Tori.

Garret took a deep breath and glanced at the man. As worship leader, he'd had more contact with the pastor on a weekly basis than most of the congregants. He'd never really opened up, but his burden was too heavy to carry alone. All of it. He'd been as strong as he knew how, and it wasn't enough. He was weak and trembling. Falling. "Can we talk?"

The pastor chuckled lightly. "Isn't that what we're doing?"

"There's more." Garret led the way across the yard and stuck a boot on a lower rung of the white fence surrounding the pasture. Trudy trotted over, and he fumbled in his pocket a moment before remembering he hadn't brought a treat for her. "Sorry, girl."

She snuffled him and stayed nearby, apparently forgiving him. If only everyone could do so as easily.

Pastor Roland rested his elbows on the top rail of the fence beside Garret, gazing out across the pasture, the canyon beyond, and the mountains in the distance. Waiting for him to talk.

"Tuck and Nancy rescued me from the system and gave me every opportunity. Tuck was an esteemed genetics professor at the University of Kentucky, and they owned a stud farm not far from Lexington. A lot of good racing stock came from his ranch."

"He's told me some stories."

"Nancy taught piano lessons. I showed promise early on, and she made sure I had the best when I'd outstripped what she could teach me. I studied music at UK and came home weekends to ride. Until I met Jenna. We were married right after graduation."

That got a reaction. Pastor Roland's head whipped to the side and his eyes widened. "You were married?" Then his voice softened. "What happened?"

"We were driving to our hotel on our wedding night,

and the car was T-boned. She died." Garret managed to keep his voice flat.

"Oh, no."

Garret tried to find comfort in the distant mountains, in the deep shadows forming along the canyon. How could he keep talking? But he had to. Someone had to know. "I went back to school to get my Masters and met another woman. I was so needy. So desperate not to be alone."

The pastor's elbows settled back to the top rail.

"Sh-she stole my compositions and pretended they were hers. She stole the career I'd been working toward. She stole more than that. She stole my trust, my hope, my faith." Garret dredged deep for courage. "That's when my parents sold out the stud farm — Dad had already retired from teaching years before — and bought this place. They came west for me, to give me a fresh start."

"Have you done that?"

The words were so quiet, Garret barely heard them over the thrumming in his ears. "I've let them down, time and time again. And now, nothing I can do will keep Nancy alive longer. She deserves a better son."

"Garret."

"Yes, sir?"

"You're a child of the one true king. Your earthly parentage has nothing to do with that. Not your birth mom, not the Morrisons. God has invited you into His family, and I believe you've accepted that invitation."

Garret nodded. Yes, he had, even though at times he felt like he was hanging on by a single strand. Just like Nancy was slipping through his fingers.

"You know that song, but it's more than lyrics and music. It's truth. We are attacked on every side by the whispers of regret and defeat, but you've been set free. You know your scriptures, son. Remember this one? 'It is for freedom that Christ has set us free; stand firm therefore, and do not submit again to a yoke of slavery.'"

"Galatians 5:1."

Pastor Roland nodded. "Walk in your truth, Garret. Walk in freedom and truth."

CHAPTER 14

I had a phone call I think you should know about." Mom met her on the steps of the small cabin Tori called home.

Must be serious, by the solemn expression on Mom's face. "Sure. Want to come in?"

"For a few minutes. I know you've been busy with that girls' school all day. All week, really. I bet you're tired."

Tori slid open the patio door to the deck overlooking the lake. "They've settled in well. By the end of next week, the place will seem empty without them here. Want a glass of iced tea? I stole a jug from Ollie."

"I'd love one. And I'm pretty sure Ollie would give you whatever you asked for."

Tori chuckled as she poured two glasses. "Okay, so I didn't steal. He keeps me supplied." The resort chef was like a favorite uncle who lived to spoil those whom he loved.

Mom settled at the tiny table beside the fridge. "It was Bonnie Briscoe. The pastor's wife."

"What's up?" At least it wasn't *her* in trouble.

"She called about Nancy Morrison." Mom picked up a couple of petals that had fallen from the wildflower bouquet Tori had set there a week ago when Denae's flowers had drooped. "It seems Nancy has aggressive pancreatic cancer. Stage four."

Tori's head buzzed as her knees weakened. She sagged into the chair opposite her mother and stared at her. This might explain so many things. "No way."

"Bonnie and Roland have known for a couple of weeks, but the Morrisons asked them to keep it quiet for a time."

And Tori had thought Garret's withdrawal had been all about her. Since when was she that important? Definitely not in the face of a parent with cancer. "Why tell us now?" And why had the pastor's wife called Mom instead of Garret? Because Tori wasn't really his friend. She'd hazard a guess even James didn't know. Had Garret kept this to himself completely?

"But it's progressing quickly." Mom inhaled sharply then let it out in a whoosh. "They can't manage on their own."

Tori remembered brushing aside Garret's mom's request to join her for coffee a few weeks back. Regret jabbed her. "Do they need someone to drive her to chemo? Or what? We can make meals." Garret couldn't cook. She'd seen his pathetic contributions to group potlucks and camping trips.

"She's refused treatment."

"But..."

"I know." Mom met Tori's gaze. "I understand it wasn't a good option for her situation. That must be hard for everyone — her *and* her men — to accept and support. I can't imagine."

How could this be? Sure, Garret's mom was pretty old, but not ancient. Cancer could be beat. Maybe not every time, but often. And that required treatment or a literal miracle. Garret's heart must be breaking.

Tori took a deep breath. "Wow. That's a blow. So, how can we help?" Not in the way she most wanted to, by wrapping her arms around Garret and holding him up.

"Gloria Delgado is going over with her housekeeper and a couple of women tomorrow to do a deep clean. Apparently, Nancy hasn't been well for several months, so more than dust on the surface needs dealing with."

"That's so like Gloria." She'd been on the front lines helping out on the Flying Horseshoe after Dad's accident, too.

"Garret hired Noela Bergstrom to exercise horses and clean stalls a few weeks ago, since Tuck also isn't well enough to run the business. That was before Garret knew of his mother's illness. I'm sure you knew about Noela."

Thanks to the grapevine, yes. Tori had spent a few minutes feeling jealous before she realized that the likelihood of a romance forming between her favorite cowboy and the widowed mother of three was extremely unlikely. She'd managed to be happy for Noela to have a job with flexible hours that she'd truly enjoy.

"Bonnie asked if I knew how to set up one of those meal trains online. I told her I'd ask you to take that on. I could probably figure it out, but you're younger and more adept on the computer."

Finally, something Tori could do to actually help. "Definitely. Does she need me to contact the church women or will the secretary handle that?"

"I didn't think to ask," Mom admitted. She took a sip of tea and met Tori's gaze. "How are you doing? It seems we rarely get a chance to talk one-on-one now that you've moved out of the house."

She wanted to brush away the question, but her mom didn't deserve that. "Struggling a bit, to be honest."

"Because of Garret?"

"How did you know?"

"I pay attention, even when my daughters don't speak."

Ouch. But Meg had been worse. "Well, yes. Partly because of him, anyway. I'm not sure why I fell for him. It's not like he ever gave me encouragement. Maybe it's normal to crush on one's big brother's best friends."

Her mother smiled. "True, but it's become more than a crush, if I'm not mistaken."

"On the contrary, it's only that. He doesn't return it, Mom. I don't think he ever will. I'm trying to think of what my future might look like without him in it, but I'm just not sure."

Mom reached across the table and covered Tori's hand. "You gave up your own dreams to help your father and me with the guest ranch. I'm sorry we asked that of you."

"It's how it was. I understood." Tori shrugged. "But, now..."

"It's not too late to fly the coop."

Tori searched Mom's face. "It seems too late. Especially when I'm not completely convinced I want to. I love it here, especially in the busy season. I love making a difference."

"Which is why you wanted to be a teacher. Is that still your dream?"

Was it? Not compared to marrying Garret. "Maybe? I wish I knew. Deb Gosselin talked to me about it just today, actually, telling me she sees my gift working with the girls. I enjoy them, but a school setting would be so limiting. Yet, what else is there? A boarding school like theirs? I can't imagine being stuck in a city like Boston. I'd be crying for home every night."

"I don't need to ask if you've prayed. I'm sure you have."

"Yes. But my... emotions... are getting in the way of hearing any answers."

"May I share this with your dad?"

It was an unnecessary question. Tori knew that telling one was the same as telling both, and it would go no further. She nodded.

"We'll pray for God's clear direction in your life. We'd sure hate to see you leave us — you're always welcome here — but we also know that, as parents, our job is to raise our children so they can leave home, be responsible adults, and give the cycle of life another push on the pedals."

If Mom knew James and Lauren were pregnant, she didn't say, so Tori didn't either. Meg already had two kids and talked of more. That left just Tori. "I'd hate to leave you in the lurch, though. An opportunity might not come with the best timing."

Mom met her gaze. "You are terrific with our guests, young and old alike, but we always have more competent applicants than we can hire. Don't cling to the old if God is calling you to the new on our account. We've tried to give you roots, but wings? You have those, too."

Tori choked up. "Thanks, Mom. I'll crack open my laptop and figure out the meal train thing. Thanks for trusting me."

If only Garret could trust her. With his heart.

CALL GARRET A CHICKEN. He'd stayed away from the house all day, seeing Gloria Delgado's SUV parked out front. His friends' mother would want to hug him, look deep in his eyes, and ask how he was holding up.

He wasn't holding up, and he didn't want to talk about it. But now her vehicle was gone and it was time for someone to start the evening meal. Maybe he'd just order pizza from Izzie's. Grab a bag of salad mix from Manahan's Grocery. Would that tempt Mom? More than the globs of overcooked pasta and value-brand canned sauce like he'd rummaged up last night. Frankly, that had been disgusting.

Garret stepped into the kitchen to the faint whiff of lemon. He'd expected the harsher odor of pine cleaner or bleach. Instead, it was more the absence of burned toast and the like. The window over the sink sparkled as sunlight angled through it, and the counters gleamed. A bouquet of summer flowers sat on the table. Even the tile floor shone with no trace of the grime that had been gathering against the cupboards' kickplates.

It would be best if he never tried to cook in this room again. If he could just preserve it exactly like this. Pizza was sounding better and better.

He crossed the space, heading for his mom's sitting room toward the back of the house, but the sound of a vehicle in the drive turned him around. Who now? A client here to ride? A visitor? Either way, it was all on him these days. And there were too many people.

The doorbell rang. Garret caught a glimpse of the visitor through the wavy glass of the door. Tori. His heart stumbled and so did his feet. No one else he knew had that short reddish-brown hair.

Oh, Lord, isn't this all hard enough?

He opened the door, but not far enough to be hospitable. "Hey."

She'd been looking out across the pasture. Now she turned to him with those beautiful eyes.

Hazel eyes with glints of green and brown and gold.

Gazing into the windows of your soul...

No. He wasn't going there.

Tori offered a tentative smile. "Hey, Garret. We heard about your mom. I'm so sorry."

He nodded. Everyone was sorry, but no one had more regrets than him and his parents.

"I brought dinner." She pointed at a slow cooker at her feet. "I know it's not much, but I hope it will help ease the day."

"Thanks." No doubt whatever was in there would be

an improvement to pizza. Not that there was anything wrong with that. He'd just had a lot of it lately.

"Do you or your parents have any food allergies or preferences?" She pulled her phone out of her pocket and opened an app. "I'm organizing a meal train for you guys, and—"

"A what?"

Tori looked up at him.

Man, he could drown in those eyes. Garret gave his head a quick shake to dislodge the lyrics.

"A meal train? It's a website created for situations like this. Someone sets it up on your behalf and lets the community know the link, and people can sign up for a day that suits them. They pledge to make a meal and bring it over. I set it up last night, called some folks from church, and we already have the next two weeks covered."

His mouth was gaping. He snapped it shut. "You don't have to—"

"Garret."

"It's too much. We don't need..." The thing was, they *did* need. That didn't mean he was ready to accept it.

"I'm not actually asking. Springs of Living Water Church loves you and your parents. You lead worship every week. Your parents have been active in so many things since you moved here. Your mom has helped out people in need. Your dad pitched in on the new roof. Don't you get it? You're part of the church community, and that goes both ways. You've given. Now it's your turn to receive."

He wanted to protest some more, but he nodded numbly.

Tori quirked a grin.

How had he not noticed she had a dimple before? Right there on her right cheek. His fingers itched to touch the indentation, but he fought the impulse. That was just too weird.

"Besides, I know you can't boil water without practically burning the house down. You may not think you need help, but Saddle Springs only has so many restaurants, and I'll hazard a guess you've already made good use of those. Was tonight going to be takeout from The Branding Iron or Izzie's Pizza?"

Garret sighed. "Pizza."

"I thought so. Garret? Be gracious, okay? Accept help. It's okay. Everyone wants to be the giver. It makes us feel like we're helping people we... care about. But for someone to give, there has to be a recipient, too. This time, it's you."

He didn't miss the hesitation in her words. What had she been about to say? Never mind. He didn't want to know. "Thank you." Wow, those had been difficult words. Words that made him feel completely powerless... which didn't change anything. He hadn't felt an iota of control since his mom's diagnosis.

"I've got a container of cookies in the car. They're oatmeal raisin." She looked down. "Your favorite. I'll grab them."

"Tori." Her name escaped his lips without permission.

She peeked up, uncharacteristically shy.

"I'm sorry." He gestured between the two of them. "I wish I had something to give you in return." Hopefully she would know he wasn't talking about cookies. "There's just nothing in me that can... fall in love."

The hazel eyes that haunted his dreams studied him. "I think you underestimate yourself."

"No." He shook his head and backed up a step, bumping into the doorjamb. "You don't really know me, Tori." This was so, so awkward. "I've got a... a background. There's just too much baggage there."

"A *background*? Everyone has one of those, Garret. If you're talking about sin in your past, isn't that why Jesus came? Why He died? So His blood cleanses us and gives us new life in Him."

Tori probably envisioned a life of drugs or wanton sex. "Consequences remain." He scrubbed his hand through his hair. "You don't understand."

"Try me."

Could he just dump his sordid past on her like that? Not a chance. Then those shining eyes would cloud over. She'd back away and reject him to protect herself. The result would be the same, but if he did the rejecting, he could protect her. At least a little.

Garret shook his head. "Tori, find some great guy to fall in love with." Hearing those words in his own voice ripped a hole in his heart. Was it really better this way? Yes. Yes, it was. "Forget about me. I'm not worth your time. Honestly."

"Do not call anything impure that God has made clean."

Acts 10:15. He recognized the words, but it was different.

Before he could react, she stepped closer. "You're worth it, Garret." And she reached up, cradled his face between her palms, and kissed him.

CHAPTER 15

I t took Tori fifteen minutes to get home. Every second of that time, she relived the feel of Garret's lips against hers. For a brief instant, he'd melded against her but then he'd stiffened and pulled back. He'd searched her face before pivoting back into the house leaving her standing there sagging off her tiptoes.

She'd left the package of cookies beside the slow cooker outside the door when she'd driven away. He'd likely come out and picked them up when she'd turned the corner out of view.

Tears still burned her eyelids as she turned into the Flying Horseshoe. How could she have been so stupid as to kiss Garret? She'd thought of little else for weeks. Months. But it hadn't lived up to her expectations at all. In her dreams, his eyes would fill with tenderness and wonder, he'd gather her close, and he'd whisper passionate words against her lips between kisses.

As if.

But at least she'd left him with no doubt where she

stood, even though her cheeks burned with embarrass-ment. She'd given him one last chance to return her love. Instead, he'd pulled back with shock and hurt and left her standing there like a fool. Just like at the wedding dance.

She exited the RAV4 to the sound of chattering girls, and gathered her dignity like a cloak around her before turning to face them.

"Did you see that cowboy's muscles?" gushed twelve-year-old Olivia. "Oh. My. Goodness."

What cowboy? They'd seen James and Matt and Lionel plenty of times and hadn't reacted quite like this. Sure, the two teen employees each had an adoring fan club tagging along behind them when activities allowed, but neither could be described as more than wiry. And the girls had mostly left James alone once they'd realized he was married. And old.

Tori scanned the ranch, her gaze landing on Noah Cavanagh's farrier truck. She couldn't help chuckling. If anyone's muscles deserved admiration, it would be the blacksmith's. It didn't hurt that he was older than Lionel and Matt but younger than James. To say nothing of cute.

Back to work then. She crossed the gravel to where Noah had parked his rig. He must have just arrived, because he was in the process of raising the sides of the truck to reveal his portable shop.

"Hey, Noah."

He glanced over, a wide grin crossing his face. "Hi, Tori." He gestured to the girls gathering around her. "What's going on this week?"

"We've got a girls school from Boston here, and I'm

pretty sure they've never seen muscles like yours close up before."

"Have, too," came Peyton's bored voice from beside Tori's elbow. "My brother's a bodybuilder. He's more built than *you*."

Noah's eyes gleamed with amusement. "Good for him." He turned back to Tori. "Hope you don't mind I came this evening instead of waiting until morning. I called your office in advance and talked to Meg. She said it was better this way, anyway, since the horses are in full use much of the day. With the long daylight hours in summer, I'm trying to get this trip to Saddle Springs wrapped up a day early."

"Sure, no worries. Did Meg talk to one of the boys about putting in some overtime?"

"Oh, man." He rubbed the back of his neck. "We didn't talk about that."

"It's okay. Can't blame a guy for wanting to take a long weekend this time of year." She sure wasn't getting any time off. Nice someone could.

"It's not that." He glanced over at the girls. "I promised my dad I'd take my sisters camping. They're about this age, and, well, kind of a handful right now."

Seeing the broad spectrum of personalities and levels of maturity in the contingent from Boston, Tori could imagine what he meant. "It's all good. Really."

The gong went for supper in the resort dining hall, and the girls surged in that direction as one unit. Lillian cast a bashful smile over her shoulder.

Noah watched them go before turning back to Tori.

"And I thought we had it bad with two. How many girls do you have here anyway?"

"Thirty. But they came with six chaperones, so the Flying Horseshoe's job is only to offer activities and food."

"Chaperones. That's what Emma and Alexia need. They're thirteen."

"Twins?"

"Yeah. I'm a twin, too. Not sure how it works, but my mom seems to throw mostly pairs."

Tori couldn't help the chuckle. "Must be fraternal twins, then?" Should she explain genetics or tease Noah about the birds and bees? Nah, she'd skip.

"Yeah. How'd you know?"

Well, he'd asked. "Because to have fraternal twins requires the woman to ovulate two eggs at a time. That predisposition runs in families. Identicals come from one egg split in two shortly after fertilization. That's not a genetic thing, just a random occurrence."

"I didn't know that. Never really thought about it, I guess. But I'd take exception to the word *random*. I prefer to believe God's in control of stuff like that."

Tori angled her head at him. "You're a Christian then?"

"Sure. You?"

"Absolutely." She studied him a moment longer. They'd never really talked before, anything beyond, *I'm done shoeing this horse; bring me another.*

"So give me some tips on how a preteen girl thinks? They're good kids, but wild as mountain lions and moody as housecats. I'm already regretting taking them camping, and we haven't even left yet. But Dad's got his hands full."

"Is your mom... gone?" Tori tried to think what she'd be like if her mom had passed away when she was that age. Man, a girl needed her mother.

Noah studied his boot scuffing in the dirt. "Not the way you think. Not dead. Not disappeared. Just depressed. Checked out."

She touched his arm. Whoa. The girls were right about his muscles. "There's nothing *just* about depression. Must be hard for everyone." She knew so little about Noah. He was a guy who came by every few weeks and looked after the horses' feet. Now, suddenly, he was becoming a three-dimensional person before her very eyes. Someone with a life outside of his visits to the Flying Horseshoe.

"Yeah. I don't get it. We're too busy for anyone to sit around and mope, you know? There's six of us guys and our two little sisters. A big spread. Not with guests, like yours." His wave encompassed the resort. "Just a busy cattle ranch. Takes our whole family to run it, even though some of us have outside work, too." His hand came to rest on the lifted wing of his truck.

"I doubt your mom thinks of it as sitting around and moping for the fun of it."

"I'm sure you're right." Noah shook his head in obvious frustration. He took a long breath. "Anyway, sorry for dumping on you. If you'd be so kind as to check whom your sister lined up to keep the horses coming, I'll get started."

"Have you had supper? Everyone's in the dining hall. No problem to set an extra plate."

He blinked. "Uh, sure. Sorry to be a bother. I don't want to take anyone away from their grub."

"Well, come on then."

Maybe she could stay busy enough to erase Garret's tormented gaze. Maybe she'd be the one to offer assistance to Noah tonight.

"THAT SMELLS GOOD." Dad shuffled into the kitchen, looking nearly as gaunt as Mom.

Should Garret be worried about both of them? He couldn't handle more than one at a time. Even one was too hard. *God, please heal her.*

"Tori Carmichael brought it by." Garret opened the slow cooker lid, allowing the beef stew aroma free access to the air. It did smell good. "I guess they started a meal train. Someone from the church will be bringing supper every day."

Dad's jaw worked. "Your mother always loved participating in ministries like that."

"Is she awake? Up to a bite of supper?"

"A bite about covers it." Dad sighed. "I'll take her a small bowl and see if she's able."

When his dad puttered out of the room with two bowls, Garret scooped up one more and sat at the table by himself. This was his future, except with takeout rather than meals from friends.

Friends?

Tori had kissed him. A sweet, innocent kiss. There'd been nothing demanding about it, not like Chantelle's. Nothing passionate, like he'd shared with Jenna.

And yet there'd been a warning in Tori's lips pressed against his. She'd waited for him long enough. She wouldn't hang around forever, letting him reject her again and again.

The first two bites had been tasty, but now the stew turned into so much compost. He pushed off from the table and stared at the container of cookies. She'd brought his favorite. She knew what he liked and cared enough to bring it.

He was crazy. What if...?

A bowl clunked on the table, and Garret turned to see Dad sinking into a seat. "You okay?"

"She's asleep." Tuck Morrison rubbed a hand across his eyes before looking up at Garret. "I'll heat some for her later if she's hungry." He pushed his own spoon through the tender meat, carrots, and potatoes in front of him. "I'm sure this is really good."

"I'm sure it is, too." Garret popped open the cookie container and carried it to the table. "Or we could go straight to dessert."

"Oatmeal raisin?" Dad's eyebrows rose as he looked between the container and Garret. "Somebody's got your number."

In more ways than one. Garret shrugged. "Tori pays attention." He snagged one and had a bite, his taste buds surging alive.

"Are you?"

"Am I what?" Garret eyed his dad.

"Paying attention. Because I think she'd like to do more than bake you an occasional batch of your favorite cookies."

Suddenly the bite he'd just swallowed became a lump of lead in his stomach. "You know I'm done with love."

"It's a good thing our heavenly Father doesn't give up so easily."

"Easily? Do I need to remind you of my track record?"

"No more than God reminds you of yours. My son, he casts your sin into the depths of the sea—"

"And puts up a *no fishing* sign. I know."

"Then why do you persist in circling your boat over that hole in the ocean?"

Garret surged to his feet. "You know why. It's not for my sake. It's to protect others."

Dad shook his head and ate a chunk of carrot. "That's not your job. God's big enough to manage the world without your help."

"How can you say that? With Mom..." He couldn't say the words.

"Son, love hurts. There's no getting around it. But so does life without love. Would I rather have lived my life alone, never knowing the beautiful woman who has loved me for over fifty years, to protect myself from the pain I'm experiencing these days? What do you think?"

Where would Garret be if Tuck and Nancy had never met, never married, never been unable to have babies of their own? How would he have fared in other foster homes? Would anyone else have seen beyond the aggressive little boy to see the torment that caused it?

He shook his head. "She's worth it."

"Son, open your heart. I don't know for sure if Tori is the right woman for you, but pray and allow God to show you."

"I don't deserve—"

"Hogwash." Dad's voice was sharp. "Life is not about what we deserve. 'The wages of sin is death, but the gift of God'... say it with me, Garret. 'The gift of God is'..."

"'Eternal life in Christ Jesus our Lord.'"

"Good. You remember. Here's another one to grab onto. John 10:10. Jesus said, 'I am come that they might have life, and that they might have it'..." Dad cupped his hand behind his ear.

"'Might have it more abundantly.'"

"Did you hear your own voice, son? God doesn't hand out Halloween-size samplers. He doesn't even hand out treats by the case. He stands us under the waterfall and pours molten chocolate over us. Abundantly."

Garret couldn't help the chuckle at the visual. "Willie Wonka style."

"Like that. More than we could ever 'ask or think, according to the power at work within us'."

"Ephesians 3:20."

"Yes, my boy. This is how you gather strength for dark days. You memorize the Word. You think on it. You absorb it into your life. Then, when you need it most, it's right there, ready to do battle in your mind."

"Because it's a two-edged sword."

Dad pointed his spoon at Garret. "There you go. Hebrews 4:12."

Garret nodded slowly. He'd been immersed in the

Word as a child. At home, at Sunday school, at Awana clubs, in private school. He'd believed, while his older brother had rebelled. Did that mean their parents shouldn't have rescued Kellen and adopted him? That loving Kellen hadn't been worth the investment?

How many people heard the love story between God and humanity and turned away? Did that mean Jesus shouldn't have come and died for their sins? That loving humanity hadn't been worth the investment?

Dad said love was worth the risk.

But Garret's heart wasn't completely convinced.

CHAPTER 16

Tori was an old hand at aiding a farrier, though she hadn't done it often in the past few years, and not at all since Noah had started working with Rusty. She could glimpse the older smith's deft hand in some of Noah's movements.

She led him horse after horse until they worked under the beam of the yard light coupled with the spotlight mounted to his truck. How many horses had he shoed today before arriving at the Flying Horseshoe? How could he even see anymore, let alone keep moving?

Finally, Noah paused and rubbed his shoulder. "Guess this one is enough for today. I can barely see straight."

"I was wondering how much longer."

"You should have said something."

"You're the one doing all the hard work. I figured I could last as long as you. The horses are enjoying the attention between the pedicure and the extra grooming while they wait their turn."

"Pedicure." Noah laughed, stretching one way then

the other before running a hand down Pippi Longstocking's flank. "You like that, girl?"

"All women do." Tori smoothed Pippi's mane. "A little pampering at the spa."

"Oh, yeah?" Noah raised his eyebrows at her in the harsh gleam of the spotlight. "I wouldn't know. It's all testosterone around Rockstead. My mother used to..." His voice trailed off.

"I'm sorry for reminding you." She studied him for a minute. "How about your sisters?"

"They're too young, thankfully."

Her eyebrows rose. "At thirteen? I doubt that unless they're super tomboys. I thought little of anything but horses at that age, but if I had a chance to go to a friend's sleepover where we did each other's nails and makeup, I took it every time."

"Then it's a good thing we live so far from town, isn't it?"

"But they have friends at school, right?"

He shook his head. "Mom homeschools them. Or she did, before things got so bad. I'm not sure they finished eighth grade."

"Aw, I feel sorry for your sisters." She just couldn't even go there with Noah's mom. "Girls that age need friends whether they're in school or not."

"We do get off the ranges for church on Sundays. That has to be enough for them. It is, for the rest of us."

Tori could just imagine two sheltered girls surrounded by six big brothers. And their big adventure was one of those cowboys taking them even further in the mountains instead of to Big Sky Waterpark or something like that? "I wish they could come here for a week or two. Maybe not when the girls school is here — they leave Friday, anyway — but there are nearly always families with kids of assorted ages here. I really feel for them."

Noah quirked a grin. "I can see how much you enjoy the girls here. You handle all their questions well. Thanks for letting them watch but keeping them occupied out of range. Big load off me knowing I didn't need to worry about them."

"They're just curious." She laughed. "And, you know, only Peyton has seen bigger muscles."

He shook his head, still grinning. "I need 'em for all this heavy work."

"I know you do."

Noah lowered one of the truck's wings and latched it. "I wish you could meet Alexia and Emma, too. They could sure do with some good influence. Someone patient like you." He eyed her thoughtfully as he rested a hand on the top of the truck box. "I'd even ask you to hire on at Rockstead Ranch if you didn't look so busy here. My stepdad would pay well to have a companion for the twins."

Tori blinked as she stared at him, her mind racing. Really? Could this be the opening she'd been praying for? A chance to get away from Saddle Springs and make a difference elsewhere? "You serious?" She kept her voice light.

"I would be if I thought you'd go for it."

"Maybe I should check it out." Tori couldn't believe she'd said that.

His eyebrows shot up. "Really? Aren't you needed here?"

In her mind's eye, Mom gave her an understanding smile and hug. Yes, Tori was good with the guests, but any outdoor-loving, extroverted Montana native could do what she did here. But helping out the Cavanagh sisters? That required someone with an affinity for thirteen-year-old girls. "I'm not indispensable here. I've been thinking of a change."

"But it's your family..."

Right. He and his five brothers worked for their dad together. He understood family, all right.

"Look, if you're serious, I'd be super grateful. I need to talk it over with Dad, of course, but I can't see why he'd object. He doesn't have enough hair left to keep pulling it out."

"Wouldn't your mom have a say, too?" Tori couldn't believe she was actually considering this impromptu invitation.

Noah slumped against the back of the truck. "You'd think. But the more she withdraws, the more Dad takes charge. If I were you, I'd run in the opposite direction, frankly. It's not just the twins. My whole family's a mess, and I can't promise one or more of my brothers wouldn't hit on you."

"I can take care of myself." The dejection in his posture and the despair in his words solidified Tori's conviction that this was something she needed to pursue. It wasn't only a desire to get away from Garret anymore. It was a door opening that could help her know if teaching might be a valid pursuit. This was more like an old-fashioned governess position, something she hadn't realized still existed in contemporary times.

"I don't doubt you can." Noah shook his head as he straightened. "And Dad wouldn't stand for that, anyway. Forget I said anything. It would never work."

"And yet you're worried about your sisters."

He rubbed the back of his neck. "Yeah. I am, but something will come up."

"Maybe something has."

Noah studied her for a minute. "Tori, you're too good for the likes of the Cavanaghs."

"You're back to do the rest of the horses tomorrow, right? Let me talk to my parents."

"You can't be serious." Yet hope lifted his voice.

"We'll see."

GARRET WINCED when he saw Lauren's orange Wrangler turn into the drive. It had, apparently, been too much to hope that Doc Torrington would come on the call just because it was for a horse not a puppy. While both veterinarians were capable, Lauren took most of the small animal calls leaving the larger ones for her senior partner.

"Hi, Garret." There was no smile on her face as she slid out of the Jeep.

"Hey." He shoved his hands into his jeans pockets. "Boomerang's in the stable."

"Wow, that's a shortage of small talk, even from you." She glowered at him. "It's been weeks since we've seen you. Since you left a message on James's cell that you were bowing off the worship team for a while and since you stopped hanging out with the gang. Since your dad is always the one opening the door when someone comes over."

Garret stared at her. "My mom's dying," he said stiffly.

"And that means you don't need friends?" Her voice softened. "We want to be here for you, but you're pushing everyone away. How can we show how much we care when your walls are this high? People need people. Even introverts, sometimes. You're not an island, Garret."

He started at that last bit. Those words took him straight back to Trevor's wedding and the song Kenny Rogers and Dolly Parton crooned at each other. Took him straight back to Tori in his arms and the hurt on her face as he'd backed off and bolted. "I don't expect you to understand."

"Try me." His best friend's wife scanned his face. "I'm not a stranger to loss, Garret. My dad died when I was a teen. It was a massive heart attack, not cancer. So, you're right, I didn't have to watch him suffer and weaken. One evening I argued with him about curfew, and the next morning he was gone. I never got to say I was sorry. Never got to say goodbye. Never got to tell him I loved him one last time."

"I-I didn't know."

"I know you didn't. You know why? Because you never let conversations get past music or horses or weather. You pretend emotions don't exist. Guess what, buddy?" She took a step closer, her eyebrows rising. "They do."

"Look, I'm sorry it annoys you that I'm a private person—"

She snorted. "Get real. You can be the Queen of Sheba for all I care. It's James you're hurting. He and Trevor and Spencer and Kade are all trying to figure out how to show you they care when you don't answer calls or texts and are conveniently invisible if anyone drives out here."

All the guys. No mention of Tori. But why would she? Unless Tori was a whole lot more talkative than Garret, Lauren wouldn't even know there might've been something between them.

It wasn't a might've been. He could deny all he wanted, but she affected him. Deeply. That kiss, right here on this doorstep, had pierced through to his heart. Why? Why couldn't he let go of his fears and reach for the gift she offered?

Take courage. That's what Pastor Roland had preached on.

Lauren turned on her heel with a grunt of annoyance. "Fine. Show me Boomerang. What's going on with him?"

Garret should feel relief that she dropped the subject, but he didn't. He needed to make the first step toward reconciling with his friends, but how? It was easier to talk horses. He swallowed hard. "His left eyelid seems swollen, and he's squinting. Dad wonders if it's a corneal ulcer."

A few minutes later she'd confirmed Dad's educated guess and given Garret instructions on how to administer the ointments over the next day or two. Lauren stopped to sweet-talk Newton and Trudy on her way out of the stable before turning to Garret in the doorway. "Have you seen Tori lately?"

He pulled back and stared at her. "I, uh, no."

"Neither have I."

Garret frowned. "But you both live at the Flying Horseshoe..."

Lauren raised her eyebrows. "She did."

"I don't understand."

"There's a lot she hasn't told me, but thank the good Lord she's not as tight-lipped as you are."

Whatever that was supposed to mean. He met Lauren's gaze and waited.

Finally, she sighed. "She's gone, Garret. She took a temporary position at Rockstead."

"Rockstead?" His mind whirled, and he grabbed at the doorframe to steady himself. "Cavanaghs' ranch?"

"One and the same."

"But she can't do that! There's how many rough-and-tumble guys out there, far from town? They'll take advantage of her. Not Noah, of course, but we don't know his brothers. And besides, Bill and Amanda need her. She leads all the trail rides and..." His voice petered off as he noticed Lauren's widening smirk. "You're messing with me."

"Sounds like it would have worked, too. But it's true. Not only is Rockstead full of testosterone-laden twenty-something single guys, those swaggering cowboys have thirteen-year-old twin sisters. Tori's good with kids, and Noah saw that in action last time he was here. Offered her a job."

"But she can't." This time his voice was weak.

"She did. Garret?" She waited until he met her gaze before she continued, her voice softer. "I'm trying to give you a break, because I know this is a really tough time for you, but this thing with Tori has been going on a lot longer. Time's running out, dude. My sister-in-law is a special person, and she doesn't deserve to be ignored and avoided by the man she loves."

Wasn't love too strong a word? More like infatuation, only that was shallow and didn't last.

Lauren must have seen the question on his face, because she sighed. "Yes, love. We don't always get to pick the direction our hearts go, Garret. I know you're hurting, but she's hurting, too. I don't blame her for grabbing the first solid opportunity to come her way and reach for her future."

"She's... dating Noah?"

Her eyebrow cocked. "What would you do about it if she were?"

Garret ran his hand through his hair and shoved his hat back on his head. His gut clenched while blood pounded in his ears. "It's up to her." He'd had his chance. She'd kissed him, and he'd walked away for her protection. That had been the best choice... hadn't it? If so, why didn't it feel like it? Why couldn't he be happy for Noah?

"What's going on inside your head, Garret? Why are you pulling away from what could be the best thing that ever happened to you? All I can think of is fear, but you've never struck me as a fearful person before. You rode out at night with Trevor and Spencer hunting a mountain lion. If that wasn't brave, I don't know what was."

He remembered that storm-filled night. "That's what friends do." Yeah, he'd been nervous. More than.

Lauren tapped his chest. "This is also what friends do. They tell each other how it is. Granted, I don't know you as well as the guys do, but you've withdrawn from them — from everyone — and, well, I'm here. So here goes."

Garret met her gaze, bracing himself.

"Whatever happened that's causing you to backpedal, whether it's your actions back then or someone else's, I am one hundred percent certain that Jesus' blood covered it on the cross. Ask forgiveness if you need to, claim it, and step into your identity as a child of God."

It sounded so simple. In some ways, it really was.

CHAPTER 17

W e're here." Tori turned off the ignition in front of her cottage. No one had minded — or at least protested — her idea to bring the twins to the Flying Horseshoe for the last half of the agreement. "Think of it like summer camp," she'd told Declan Cavanagh.

Now there was an intimidating man. *Type A* might as well be branded on his forehead. The entire Rockstead Ranch thrummed with focused energy with little interaction and even less grace. No wonder Declan's wife withdrew, his sons worked like a tightly tuned machine, and his daughters kept their escapades to themselves.

Tori had signed on for a month, but two weeks on the remote ranch with two bored young teens was more than enough. But could she even pull off chaperoning the girls at the resort? She'd be helping out at the same time, but tourists were a piece of cake compared to twins.

Emma and Alexia slid out of either side of the RAV4, and the doors shut with twin slams.

Tori leaned on the vehicle, watching the girls take in the Flying Horseshoe. It was early afternoon, and a small group had gathered over by the corrals. They'd soon be heading out on a trail ride. On the other side of the row of cottages lay the small lake. A few teen girls sunbathed while smaller kids built sand castles with parents. Several boys shot water guns at each other from the unicorn and flamingo floaties beyond the raft. Two orange kayaks nosed along the far shore.

The tension in Tori's shoulders began to ease at the welcome, familiar sights.

Alexia crossed her arms over her chest. "It doesn't look too awful."

High praise.

"Can we swim?" Emma gathered her long hair and tossed it over her shoulder.

"Sure. Let's haul our stuff in and get you settled first, then you can hit the lake." Tori popped open the hatch, and the girls reached for their luggage. Carrying everything inside was going to take more than one trip, since Tori had also packed for a month away.

She led the way up the steps along the cabin to the deck overlooking the little lake then set her burdens down to open the slider into the living area. Beyond lay the kitchen, bath, and a small bedroom with a loft above them.

Tori pointed at the log staircase on the left. "You two will be up there. Make yourselves at home." Hopefully Mom had sent someone to set up the two cots Tori had asked for.

Emma headed for the steps, hoisting her wheeled

luggage, with Alexia right behind her. A minute later she called down, "Sweet view!"

Tori grinned. With the tall windows facing the lake, she knew what the girl meant.

"Where's our bathroom?" asked Alexia.

"Down here. We'll share."

A mutter followed by a thud told Tori what the teen thought of that. Well, the Carmichaels didn't have the Cavanaghs' money or their mansion. If anything proved wealth didn't make people happy, the Cavanagh family provided the object lesson. Two weeks at Rockstead had served a good reminder that she had a really good life here at home, lack of romance notwithstanding. Noah and his brothers might be good-looking and nice enough, one at a time, but none of them held a candle to Garret Morrison.

She carried her own bags into her small main-floor space and dumped them on the bed before returning to the SUV to grab another load.

"Hey, sis! Need a hand there?" James slung his arm across her shoulders and gave her a light squeeze. "Good to see you."

Tori turned into her brother's embrace. "You, too, James. It's good to be home."

He poked his chin toward the cottage. "Your charges inside?"

"Yep, and already complaining about three of us sharing a bathroom." She rolled her eyes. "You should see their mansion. It makes our parents' house look like a mountain cottage. It's way bigger than even Delgados' house at Eaglecrest."

James chuckled. "Well, the Cavanaghs have eight kids and the Delgados only had three, so I imagine they needed more space."

"Kind of, but they're a blended family, and I think the house is older than that."

"Meaning?" His eyebrows rose.

"Well, they each had three boys when they married, and the girls belong to both of them." Although it truly seemed the girls belonged to all the brothers but neither parent. Tori couldn't wrap her head around their family dynamics.

"Huh." James slung a backpack over one shoulder and lifted two suitcases. "What's in these? Gold bricks?"

Tori laughed. "One is full of about eight pairs of riding boots. A choice for every outfit."

"Girls." The word was without condemnation. James headed for the cottage while Tori grabbed the rest of the stuff. She'd just stepped up onto the back deck when a screech came from within.

"There's a man in here!"

She jogged inside. "Just my brother. Sorry!" She hadn't even stopped to wonder if the girls might be in the midst of changing into their swimsuits. Not to worry, though. They were fully clothed as they leaned over the log rail above, eyes wide at the sight of a red-faced James setting their bags down just inside the door.

Tori stifled a giggle, remembering how the girls from Boston reacted to Noah. "Girls, meet my big brother, James. He and his wife, Lauren, live around the end of the lake. James, that's Alexia on the left and Emma on the right."

Emma gave a little wave.

"Hi, girls." James's gaze shifted between them as he lifted a hand in acknowledgment. "Brought in the rest of your stuff."

"Thanks." Alexia dragged out the word.

James shot Tori a sheepish grin as he pivoted for the exit.

She could hardly blame him. "Okay, grab your things from down here and finish putting them away." She made a show of checking her watch. "We can head over to the beach in about half an hour. I hope you brought plenty of sunscreen."

Emma scampered down the stairs with her sister following more sedately. "Are there cute guys closer to our age? And, you know, not married?"

"I'm not sure what we've got for guests this week, but remember your manners."

Alexia rolled her eyes. "We're always good."

Emma giggled.

"I can send you back to Rockstead, you know," warned Tori. That would be a last resort, though. Her heart had truly gone out to the twins who only seemed to be in the way at home... when they were noticed at all.

Emma saluted. "Promise we'll behave."

They'd get their chance to prove it at James and Lauren's joint birthday party tonight. And Tori would get her chance to see Garret again. For better or for worse.

"ARE YOU SURE YOU'RE OKAY?" Garret looked from one parent to the other.

Mom lay in the hospital bed they'd rented for her studio. The head was raised a little tonight, but she still looked small and wan in its white shroud.

Dad sat at her side in a wing chair with his worn leather Bible on his lap. He met Garret's gaze. "Go on, son. Have a good time."

"You'll let me know if you... if you need me."

"Of course. But we'll be fine here."

With a sharp nod, Garret headed out of the sick room. *Why, God?* The words were a constant refrain these days. Sure, it might be deemed a pity party, but it wasn't just for his own sake. It was for Nancy's sake. And, yes, he'd noticed he thought of his parents more often as Nancy and Tucker recently than he had for years, like he was separating himself from them already, trying to lessen the impact losing them would have.

He ducked into his red pickup. There would have been no way he'd attend his friends' party if Tori were still around, although Lauren probably wouldn't have taken no for an answer regardless. She'd badgered a promise out of him when she'd returned to assess Boomerang's progress. Said it was high time he opened up and let his friends support him in this troublesome time.

She was probably right. That didn't make the short drive to the Flying Horseshoe much less daunting, though. All the rest of the gang made up half his anxiety.

Garret passed the main gates of the guest ranch. The place looked peaceful with the evening sun glinting off the water and lights on in some of the cottages. A few stragglers headed toward the dining hall past horses grazing in the pasture.

Then it was only the lake beside Creighton Road for a minute or two then the road that forked to Eli and Meg's and James and Lauren's. He pulled in, parked behind Trevor's black truck, and levered himself out.

"Morrison!" yelled Kade. "Good to see you, man."

Garret waved in acknowledgment. They'd better not make a big deal of him being here, or he'd make an excuse to leave sooner rather than later. He walked past the house toward the gazebo lit with strings of solar lights, his towel draped around his neck. Lauren had assured him the ranch chef, Ollie, was sending over the food, and there was nothing Garret needed to bring but himself.

The spread looked magnificent, as usual. He'd had his fill of pasta and casseroles the past couple of weeks. Meal trains had their place, and he was grateful to the church women, but couldn't they lighten up their offerings?

"Hey." A heavy hand clouted Garret's back and he turned to see Sawyer Delgado.

"Hi there." Garret nodded at the youngest brother, who showed up at random between rodeo events. Might as well try to be friendly. "How're things?"

"Can't complain. Won a couple of events down in Wyoming last week, second in some others. You?"

Garret's throat choked. "Okay." If there was anyone he didn't want to discuss his mom's illness with, Sawyer would hit the top of the list.

He scanned the group on the dock and in the lake, where Cheri was doing her best to dunk Kade. And failing. Maybe he could relax a smidge. Tori wasn't here. He knew she wouldn't be, but he'd still been torn between hope and dread on the way over. It wasn't like he'd forgotten for an instant what her lips had felt like under his.

"Hey, have you met Adam Cavanagh? Buddy of mine from the circuit." Sawyer thumbed to the guy coming up beside him. "Adam, this is Garret Morrison. Owns a riding stable."

Automatically, Garret reached to shake the man's hand. "Related to Noah?"

Adam grinned. "He's my kid brother. I see he's made his mark around here."

"He's a good farrier. Pleasure to meet his brother."

"Yeah, he's done good." Adam looked around. "Nice spot here."

"Sure is."

Sawyer pointed out to the lake. "Looks like some of the tourists got lost."

A canoe with three paddlers angled its way toward the nearby dock.

"Crashing the party?" asked Adam, turning to look.

Sawyer laughed. "Maybe word got out. I guess James will tell them to get lost if that's what it is."

Garret shook his head slightly, not that anyone was paying attention. James would be more likely to invite them in for cake and ice cream. As he watched, his eyes narrowed. If he didn't know better, he'd think the paddler in the stern was Tori. But wasn't she a couple of hours away at Rockstead?

"You've got to be kidding me!" Adam jogged down the slope and out onto the dock.

Of course. If it were Tori — and his eyes had not deceived him — the Cavanaghs would all know her. Garret had all but pushed her straight at that family of six macho cowboys. He had no one to blame but himself.

The stern paddler expertly turned the canoe against the side of the dock away from the swimmers, but it was the middle person Adam hauled out and hugged, then the front one.

"What's going on?" Denae Delgado asked from nearby.

Garret glanced at her. That's what he wanted to know. Because he was quite, quite sure that Tori Carmichael was climbing out of the canoe and tying its bowline to a post on the dock. She wasn't at the Cavanaghs' ranch. If his guess was correct, she'd brought her charges back to the Flying Horseshoe, only to be greeted by their big brother, Adam. A rodeo rider like Sawyer.

Garret pivoted on his heel only to slam right into James. "Excuse me."

But James grabbed his arm. "Where are you going?"

"Home." He choked the word out.

His friend glanced out to the lake then riveted on Garret. "Didn't think you were chicken, Morrison."

"You guessed wrong."

Humor flicked through James's eyes then fled. "Don't be so hard on yourself. Or on anyone."

"Lauren lied to me."

James's eyebrows rose as his eyes narrowed. "Pardon me?"

"Okay, not in so many words, but she led me to believe Tori was away."

"She was. We didn't know she was coming home, bringing the twins with her, until last night. She arrived this afternoon. I'm sorry we forgot to send up a smoke signal to let everyone know." Sarcasm laced his words.

Garret took a deep breath and met James's eyes. "I'm sorry. That accusation was uncalled for."

James snatched the truck key that had been dangling from Garret's fingers. "You're forgiven. You're also staying."

"James..."

"Go jump in the lake, Morrison. That's what all the cool kids are doing. All your friends. Remember friends?" James waved a hand around the gathering. "This is what they look like. We're going to swim and eat and shoot up some fireworks. After that, I'll give you your keys back. Meanwhile, I think I'll drop them in my wife's underwear drawer. Pretty sure that will keep you from digging for them." He winked and turned for the house.

For a brief instant, Garret entertained the thought of challenging his friend for that keyring, but James was probably tougher than he was. Besides, why make a scene? He was here now, and he might as well make the best of it.

Down on the dock, Tori Carmichael looked straight toward him and waved.

There was no avoiding her.

CHAPTER 18

Tori ripped her attention away from Garret and back to the brawny cowboy embracing her charges.

He had a twin clinging to each arm as he turned toward her, curious eyes taking her in. "Hi. I'm Adam Cavanagh. How do you happen to have my sisters?"

"She's our nanny," Emma said with a giggle as her bare feet regained the planks.

"Nanny?" His eyebrows shot up. "Isn't that for little kids?"

Alexia gave Tori a disdainful look. "Daddy figured we needed a keeper, and this is what happened. Noah offered her a job and Dad agreed. Now we have someone watching us twenty-four-seven. Rescue us, Adam!"

He laughed, a pleasant enough sound. "Dad's got your number, Alexia. It's about time he did something about you."

"I'm Tori Carmichael. The Flying Horseshoe is my parents' ranch. After spending a couple of weeks at Rockstead, your father allowed me to bring the twins here for a bit. It's just a one-month contract." And one she had little desire to renew, much as her heart went out to the girls.

He nodded at her, hands still claimed by his sisters. "I'm a friend of Sawyer's and came home with him for a couple of days between events." His gaze trailed down her body and back to her face. "What a surprise to find Alexia and Emma here, and to meet you. I'm very glad I came."

She'd nearly left her shorts and tank top at the cabin. Thankfully she'd figured she might want them as the evening cooled off later, because *whew* for the additional barrier from this guy's appreciative once-over.

"I see you two have met." Sawyer nudged Adam. "She's a cutie, isn't she?"

That did it. Tori narrowed her eyes at Sawyer. "Stuff it, Delgado. Did you forget you already had a girlfriend? Or did you ditch Anna already?"

He frowned. "She's the reason I came home this weekend, but she's not picking up my calls. You seen her lately?"

"I've been away for two weeks. I haven't seen anybody until tonight."

"I stopped by The Branding Iron, but she wasn't working, and the kid who was on didn't have time to check the schedule. It was hopping in there."

"It's Thursday."

He rolled his eyes. "Brilliant, my dear Watson."

"Anna always works on Thursdays."

"Well, she's not there tonight."

Maybe she'd figured out what a jerk Sawyer was and was avoiding him. Better late than never.

"Come swimming," Emma begged, tugging on Adam's arm.

"Sure. That's what I came for. That and food." He winked at Tori. "And for pleasant surprises."

Men. "Go ahead," Tori told the girls, not that they were waiting for her approval. "I'll take the cooler Ollie sent up to the gazebo and join you in a minute."

"I'll get it." Sawyer leaned into the canoe. "What did you bring? It looked like a full spread up there already."

She laughed. "When Ollie sent all that, he didn't know we'd have teen girls. He figured he needed to provide them with suitable snacks, too. I think there are pigs-in-blankets and chocolate cookies. The non-baked kind."

"Mm. My favorites, too." Sawyer carried the cooler down the dock then toward the gazebo.

Tori walked beside him, which had nothing to do with Garret still standing right where he'd been for the past five minutes, just catching the glow of the gazebo's lights, and everything to do with arranging the additional snacks according to Ollie's directions.

"If being an adult means I don't get any of Ollie's cookies, I'll pull a Peter Pan and stay a kid."

She angled a look up at Sawyer. "Thought you'd already made that decision."

"You wound me." He winked and leaned closer, nudging her. "I'm very grownup in some ways."

If she was supposed to ask what those were, he had another think coming. "It creeps up on all of us, one way or the other," she agreed, shifting away. Like now. Taking on the Cavanagh twins had taught her a couple of things. One, caring for someone else's teens full-time was not a task to be taken lightly, and two, she really missed the daily routines of the Flying Horseshoe.

It wasn't Garret she missed. She missed home. That was all. Right?

Sawyer set the cooler down, and she bent to flip it open and remove the containers.

He reached for them. "Where do you want them?"

"I can do it." Why couldn't he take the hint and just leave her alone? Alone but for Garret standing like a fence post a few feet away.

"I don't mind."

"Sawyer, really. Go swimming with your friend. Just remember those girls are thirteen. You better not flirt with them."

"Me?" He pressed a hand over his heart.

For the first time, she realized he was shirtless. And kind of sculpted... which wasn't much of a turn-on in the face of his assuming attitude. "Get out of here. I'm serious."

"All right, then. Come on down to the lake so I can throw you in."

"As if. And aren't you mourning Anna, if she's avoiding you?"

Sawyer shrugged. "Her loss."

Tori gritted her teeth as he strutted off then turned to say hi to Garret. Only he wasn't there anymore. Or anywhere she could see.

GARRET TOSSED a pebble into the tumbling creek not far from the group gathered by the gazebo and dock. He could only hope no one would find him while he pulled himself together. At least his swim trunks and T-shirt were dark and the creekside shadowed by the log footbridge.

She was more beautiful than he remembered. The short auburn hair suited her face, making her look like a pixie. He'd seen her trim shape a hundred times, but never had her gentle curves looked so tempting as tonight in short jean cutoffs and a light green tank top crested with the guest ranch's symbol, a winged horseshoe. And now even more skin was exposed in a two-piece suit that flashed slivers of her belly. If he held her in his arms, he'd touch her skin there, at the curve of her waist.

But it was her lips he craved. He'd tasted them once. What had he been thinking, savoring them even briefly that day on his doorstep? For five seconds he'd given in to what might have been. Five seconds that had branded his heart as surely as a cowboy's hot iron branded the flank of a calf, and with the same result. Ownership had been marked.

His heart was Tori's. His parents encouraged him to go for it. Could he?

He looked toward the lake, where dusk had settled and someone had lit a couple of gas lanterns on the dock posts, casting a warm glow over the moonless scene.

Adam Cavanagh stood on the planks and reached to

give Tori a hand up beside him. She was laughing. Just as she'd laughed with Adam and Sawyer earlier.

She'd obviously moved on, and Garret couldn't blame her. At best, he'd sent her mixed signals. At worst, he'd turned away from her, shunning the gift she offered him. One of those times had been public, and still she'd come again.

And kissed him.

He touched his mouth now as he watched her shove Adam off the dock. Would she kiss Adam tonight? She wouldn't. It had taken her five years to kiss Garret, but then again, he'd never encouraged her. Flirted with her. Not like Cavanagh was doing right now. The guy clambered back onto the dock, and Tori dove in. With strong, sure strokes, she headed along the shore.

Toward him. He sank deeper into the shadows. With any luck he'd stay camouflaged.

"Garret?" Her voice was pitched to his ears alone, to be heard over the tumbling creek.

So much for his hope.

For a long moment, Tori thought her eyes had deceived her. There hadn't been much to the slight movement by the bridge, but she'd been scanning the shore in between dives, and there'd been a definite flicker down this way.

"Hey."

Her heart sped as she sloshed ashore over the slippery rocks. "Whatcha doing over here?" As if she didn't know.

His shoulder lifted in a shrug.

She wouldn't have seen the movement if she wasn't so tuned to him. A wide rock parted the creek not far from where Garret sat. She settled onto it, shivering slightly from the cooler water. "How's your mom doing?"

"Not very well."

She'd heard as much from her own mother. "I'm sorry to hear that."

"It's hard. On Dad."

"On you, too."

He turned to look out on the lake. "Yeah, well. It's just how it is."

How could she encourage him to accept emotion? It wasn't just for her, but he needed it for himself, too. For the time remaining with his mom. "Tell me about her. Are you close?" They had to be, for him to be hit this hard, but she couldn't think of a better opener.

"You mean for an adopted kid?" The pain sprang from his voice.

She held back the surprise. How had she known him for five years but not known something this basic about him? She'd bet James didn't know, either. "How old were you?"

"Four."

"So you remember it."

He gave a sharp nod. Her eyes had adjusted to the shadows enough to see his clenched jaw.

Lord, help me speak Your words. "I don't think your parents could love you more if you'd been born to them."

"It's true."

She waited.

"Have you watched anyone die?"

Tori shook her head. "Not a person. An animal or two, when I was a kid."

"I have."

She absorbed that. Did he want her to ask him who? But then, suddenly, she knew. "Your mom?"

His jaw clenched, and his stare out on the water seemed blank. "Drug overdose. I begged her to wake up. I was hungry and afraid."

"I'm sorry." If he were nearer, she'd touch him, but he'd push her away. Again. Best if she stayed put out on this rock.

"She'd been dead for three days when someone came."

Tori closed her eyes and tried to think what a horrific three days that must have been for a terrified four-year-old. It wasn't that long ago that her nephew had been that age. Her heart broke for little-boy Garret. "I can't imagine." But it might explain a thing or two about the man he'd become.

"I was one of the lucky ones." His voice was quiet, expressionless. "The Morrisons took me in as a foster kid and adopted me soon after, since no one claimed me."

"Your dad?"

Garret shrugged. "Unknown."

"God was looking after you," she said softly.

"I believed that for a lot of years."

Tori drew her legs up and wrapped her arms around her knees. His words chilled her heart. "When did you stop?" *And when did you start again?* Because he believed now, didn't he?

"When my wife died."

What? Tori swayed on the rock, feeling blood leave her brain, leaving behind a pounding lightheadedness. She stared at him. "You've been keeping more secrets than I ever dreamed of."

His eyes locked onto hers, and the pain in them blasted through the air and seared her, too. "We'd been married three hours. We were on our way to the hotel when a drunk T-boned my car. Jenna was killed instantly."

Jenna. Garret had had a wife, and her name was Jenna. Garret'd had an entire past before Saddle Springs. He'd been *married*. Not for long, but long enough to count. Three hours. Tori shook her head, trying to absorb his blunt, emotionless words. "I'm sorry, Garret."

"I struggled with my faith for a couple of years. Then... something else happened. Not something I wish to talk about."

Obviously, he didn't want to talk about any of it but, for some reason, he was telling her tonight. Why?

"I didn't see a future back east. My parents — the Morrisons — bought Canyon Crossing."

Wait, they'd come here because of whatever had happened to Garret? Something that wasn't his wife's death? How much had this man been through and kept to himself? At least his parents had been there for him. Tori hadn't missed that he'd felt he needed to clarify who they were.

"It's been good here. Pouring myself into the stables, into the church, has been therapeutic for me."

There was an unspoken *but* at the end of that. Her

heart sank. "Are you moving away? You and your dad? After your mom..." His dad was pretty old, too.

Garret shook his head. "I don't know. Tori, don't you see? I don't know anything. I don't know who I am. I don't have a whole heart to give anyone." He focused on her once again. "I'm still that little kid who watched his mom die. Still the young groom who saw that car coming a split second before the crash. Saw the shock on Jenna's face as she died. I thought there'd been some healing since then — it's been over eight years since that day — but put me in a tough spot like Mom's cancer, and I realize the wound has been festering all this time. Not healing."

Tori couldn't handle being on the cold, solitary rock by herself. Not when Garret needed a human touch, whether he knew it or not. She sloshed through the few feet of water and reached toward him.

He shot to his feet and stood looking down at her.

Her hands dropped to her sides as she gazed back, pinned by the torture in his eyes.

"That's why I can't love, Tori. Not because I don't want to. Not because I don't have... feelings." He swallowed hard. "But for your sake. You're beautiful. Trusting. You have a lot to give the right man, but I'm not him. I've been nothing but a mess of pain from childhood on, and everyone around me suffers with me. I can't do that to you."

She stepped closer so the heat of his body warmed hers down the length of it. "Can't? Or won't take a chance? God's bigger, Garret. He's bigger than your mess. Bigger than mine."

"You don't have a mess." Garret's finger slid down her cheek, leaving a tingling burn in its wake. "You're innocent. Perfect."

"I'm so not perfect."

"What have you got compared to me?"

Tori caught his hand and threaded her fingers through his. "I've got faith. I've got love. And I *know* Jesus is enough to get us through. I know He heals us when we're broken. Gives strength when we are weak. He's *enough*, Garret."

She slid her other hand around his waist and held his stiff body until it relaxed slightly and he pulled her close.

Lord, please don't let me make a mistake here. But I know You're bigger than Garret's past. Please, please heal him. Not for my sake, but his and Yours.

Tori tilted up her head to look at Garret, marveling in the secure hold he had around her. And then his face angled toward hers, and his mouth crushed on top of hers.

CHAPTER 19

Garret gave himself a moment to savor the possibility of his future as Tori slid her arms around his neck and melded her body against his, kissing him back as though she trusted him not to hurt her again.

He pulled away slightly. "Tori, I—"

She feathered her lips across his jaw, stealing his voice. "Less talking, more kissing, cowboy."

"I'm a mess, Tori."

"We already covered that." She cradled his face between her hands and looked deep into his eyes.

Hazel eyes with glints of green and brown and gold.
Gazing into the windows of your soul,
Everything you think is mirrored there—
I'm powerless against you;
I'm drowning in you...

More lyrics erupted in his brain like fireworks, and this time they brought a simple melody with them. Garret gathered Tori close, willing the moment to remain forever.

A small part of him stayed anchored in the reality of the July evening. Of splashes and laughter and the sound of a vehicle shutting off. Of the fragrance of mossy rocks and clear mountain streams and the sweet scent of the woman in his arms. Of the taste of her mouth caressing his.

Garret groaned, pushing aside the certain knowledge that he was going to regret this. More to the point, Tori was going to. But that moment was not this one. This moment filled all his senses and smoothed the rough edges of his spirit. This moment gave him hope and strengthened his faith. Could it be that God was done punishing Garret for his past sins? Maybe Dad was right, that God wanted to give him abundant life even here on earth as well as eternity.

He could taste that promise on Tori's lips, on her sweet jaw and soft throat that pulsed against his seeking mouth.

"Garret..." she breathed. "I can't believe this is real. Tell me I'm not dreaming."

Was it real? It sure felt real. With every second he spent kissing this delectable woman, he felt more grounded. Like he was coming home at last.

"*Adam!*"

Garret stilled at the female voice. He knew that voice, and it wasn't from Saddle Springs. It was from his past, and the trickle of icy water at the sure knowledge this moment was too good to last became Niagara, thundering over him.

Chantelle Devereaux. He'd last seen her headed for Nashville. What was she doing in Montana? He remembered the flyer. The tour. He'd looked up her Youtube channel to see stadiums filled with screaming fans jumping and clapping and belting out the lyrics with her. Lyrics to his compositions.

He put his hands on Tori's arms and pushed her away. Not hard, but enough that she slipped on the mossy rock. He steadied her, his breathing rough, not just from kissing but from shock.

"Garret?" she whispered, looking up at him. "What's wrong?"

He looked around wildly. No, they were definitely in the shadows. He could barely make Tori out, even with her pale exposed skin. Eyes accustomed to the lights illuminating the party would not be able to see into the shadow.

The question repeated in his mind, growing louder until it thundered. Why was Chantelle here at James and Lauren's birthday party of all places?

Tori gave him a little shake. "Garret! What's going on?"

He could see why she wondered. One minute he'd been pouring his passion into her and the next, he'd frozen in place. "No," he whispered. "No."

She took a step back, her hands dropping. "You can't do this to me. You can't ignore me for years then kiss me like that and then push me away. You can't do it, Garret. That's not how this works."

A chill seeped into him from the skin inward. Tori. He

sought her face, her features in the darkness. "I'm sorry." His voice was ragged. Broken.

"Sorry for what? For kissing me? For allowing yourself to feel emotion? And, horror of horrors, to actually express it?" Her arms crossed over her chest.

"No. Yes. I'm sorry. I tried to warn you."

Her finger jabbed at his shoulder. "You're not making a lick of sense, Garret Morrison." Her voice rose.

"Shh. Don't let them hear." Don't let Chantelle hear.

"You don't want anyone to know we kissed? I've got news for you, buddy. They're not that stupid. They know you and I are both missing from the group. I told Adam to keep an eye on the twins for a bit, that I'd be back. You think no one knows we have a thing for each other, just because you've tried to pretend it doesn't exist?" She shoved him again, harder.

Garret slid off the rounded rock and milled his arms to catch his balance. When he regained his footing, he heard Tori crashing through the bushes beside the creek. "Tori, don't."

"Forget it, Garret. I can't believe I was this stupid. When will I ever learn? I'm thinking right now is a good time." Her feet gained the dirt footpath.

He strained, but couldn't hear her steps. A moment later, he heard Lauren say, "You okay?" and Tori's grunted response.

Garret sank to the mossy rock and cradled his head in his hands. His past had collided with his future, and the past had won. He'd known it was too much to hope for that he could ever get past it. Right in this moment when he'd taken a chance, dumped his story on Tori and then kissed her? That's when reality had to slap him upside the head?

Lord, why aren't you helping me? I've been feeling like You don't notice me anymore. That You've forgotten me. You don't love me. And if You wanted me to feel differently, it couldn't have been that hard for an all-powerful God to keep Chantelle far from my new life in Saddle Springs.

He needed to disappear without being seen, but James had confiscated his truck keys, and Lauren's underwear drawer was definitely off limits.

The other alternative was to take courage. As if he knew where to find it.

Tori's MIND reeled as she tried to pull herself together. Left to her own devices, she'd pull a Garret maneuver and slip away. Head to the cottage, crawl into bed, and pull her comforter over her head until she could bear to emerge, if that ever happened.

But, she couldn't. She was responsible for two teens, even though she'd dumped them on their older brother for a bit. When she left this party, Alexia and Emma were coming with her. Since James had just added logs to the fire and Lauren and Cheri were removing covers from the food, it was unlikely she could convince the twins their part in the evening was over. There'd be a scene, and that would make the situation worse than it already was.

If *worse* was a possibility. Which was doubtful. She'd

done it again. Pushed Garret's buttons until he reacted. His reaction had been all she could have dreamed of, at least for a few minutes. And then he'd thrust her away. What had come over him this time?

Tori sidled around the gazebo and came in the side furthest from the creek, trying to make a quiet entrance.

Her sister-in-law shot her a questioning look. "You okay?"

The best she could come up with was a noncommittal sound and a quick headshake.

Lauren leaned closer and lowered her voice. "What happened?"

"Garret happened."

"Good or bad?"

Tori closed her eyes for a second and felt herself swaying. "Both." Her voice choked. "But bad wins."

"I'm so sorry." Lauren gave her a swift hug. "Do you want to talk about it? We can go over to the dock or even inside."

"It's your party. Enjoy it." Tori glanced around the group, looking for the twins. Best to start acting like the grownup she was. Her gaze fell on a curvy blonde attached to Adam Cavanagh. She looked vaguely familiar, but Tori couldn't place her. She frowned and nudged Lauren. "Who's that?"

Her sister-in-law's face brightened. "You're never going to believe it! She's Chantelle Devereaux, the famous singer!" Lauren's hands fluttered, and her voice filled with awe. "It's complicated, I guess, but she and Adam are dating, and she had an unexpected day off the western tour and came to catch up with him. I just can't believe *Chantelle Devereaux* is at my house!"

"Wow, that's really cool. Do you have any albums or CDs she could sign for you?"

"We buy all our music digitally. If I'd known, though..." Lauren sighed.

Chantelle smiled up at Adam, who curled his arm possessively around her shoulders. She was wearing a sheer low-cut top and shorts that made Tori's swim bottoms look positively old-ladyish.

The twins looked singularly unimpressed. They sat beside the fire pit giving their brother occasional disgusted looks. Maybe Tori would be able to get them home early, after all. She cut toward them past Cheri and Denae.

"Did you hear the news?" Cheri asked. "Carmen had the baby late this afternoon."

Tori pivoted toward her friends. "She did? On James and Lauren's birthday?"

"I know, right? A baby boy. Jackson Howard Haviland." Cheri held out her phone with a photo of a smiling Carmen holding a newborn.

"Look at that sweetie. Eight pounds, three ounces," Denae said with a grin. "Trevor says Spencer is over the moon."

"I'm so happy for them. I bet Juliana is excited, too." Tori glanced from the phone to the twins. "Maybe I'll take the girls out to see them in a few days when they've settled in a bit."

"I'm sure they'd like that."

Alexia's elbow jabbed her sister, and Emma shoved back. Great.

"Excuse me. Duty's calling." Tori walked over and settled on the bench beside Emma. "You guys having fun? Or ready to call it a night?"

"I don't like her," Emma announced, rather too loud, casting a glare toward the celebrity.

"We haven't even eaten yet." Alexia crossed her arms.

"We could go right after food." Tori yawned. "I'm getting tired."

Alexia narrowed her gaze. "I don't think so. Isn't there supposed to be fireworks, too?"

"We could watch those from our deck across the lake." But Tori could feel the argument weakening.

"You said," Emma countered. "Isn't this party the reason we came here from Rockstead?"

Tori let out a long breath. "Yep, you're right. It's just the day is catching up with me." She knew when she was losing. "If you guys want to stay, we can. Until the fireworks are done."

The fireworks were already definitely over. It was amazing no one else seemed to have noticed the explosions going on over by the creek a bit ago, but then they'd fizzled to nothing in two seconds flat. What was going on in Garret's brain? She couldn't begin to imagine. Sure, he'd had a traumatic childhood and a tragic wedding day, but he'd found peace in the meanwhile.

"Anyone seen Garret?" asked Trevor. "His truck is here, but I haven't seen him."

"He's around somewhere." James looked straight at Tori across the group, and his eyebrows hiked.

She gave a tiny shrug. So not going there.

"Garret. Now that's an unusual name. I used to date a

guy named Garret. One of the best musicians I've ever known." Chantelle batted her eyes at Adam. "But he sure didn't have muscles like yours."

Emma jabbed her finger toward her mouth in a gagging motion.

Tori managed not to snicker.

"Sounds like our Garret," Lauren offered. "He's been leading worship in our church most Sundays for five years."

"Well, I'll be. That's about when I lost touch with Garret Morrison."

The air seemed to shimmer as though time stood still between two worlds.

"Garret Morrison?" Trevor asked at last, breaking the charged silence. "Where did you know him?"

Chantelle looked around the group as though gauging the response. "Lexington, Kentucky. We were both in the music program at UK." Somehow her gaze landed on Tori and held. "We were... very close. He even asked me to marry him, but we had some differences, you know?"

There was no doubt that they were all talking about the same Garret Morrison. The man who'd dumped bombshells a few minutes ago about the deaths of two women he'd loved, but had somehow failed to mention this major relationship. A rejected proposal.

He'd kissed Tori then pushed her away. Was he trying to find out what it felt like to be the one in control of ending things? Sounded like he'd had little experience with that. Until tonight.

Tori blinked as her eyes focused on the man leaning

against a tree just beyond the lighted gazebo. Garret stood, arms crossed over his chest.

His presence seemed to register with everyone else in the same moment as others turned in his direction.

"Hey, Chantelle. Long time no see. What are you doing here?"

CHAPTER 20

Chantelle nestled closer to the big cowboy at her side even as her eyes widened. "Garret! Well, I'll be. I never dreamed I'd see you here, so far from home."

"Saddle Springs is my home. These are my friends." Garret pinned Adam Cavanagh with a stare. "Other than your new boyfriend, whom I've never met before tonight. You should know, Adam, that she uses men as stepping stones to get what she wants."

She straightened somewhat and let out a small laugh. "Bless your heart, Garret. You're always so melodramatic." She glanced around the group, probably to gauge the way others reacted. "Just because you didn't get your way with me back then."

Garret stared at her. "You stole from me. You passed off my compositions as your own. You took the job you knew I wanted under false pretenses. Don't make it sound like I was only after your body. I loved you. Trusted you."

He didn't dare take the group's measure. Didn't dare

see the disappointment on Tori's face. It didn't matter, anyway. He'd pushed her away again and again. Now she was learning the final piece to his sordid puzzle. His gullibility and patheticness was an open book for all to read.

"I've got a successful music career now. Not because of you, sugar, but because of my own talent and hard work."

Garret gritted his teeth. "You are gifted. I'll grant you that. But it wasn't your talent that opened the first door. It was mine." He probably sounded like a pouty little kid demanding his share of credit and attention.

"I'm sorry you see it that way." Chantelle rose, tugging Adam up with her. "Come on, cowboy. This isn't the warm welcome I expected. Let's go find somewhere else to hang out."

Adam looked uncertainly at his sisters, who stared between him and Chantelle with wide eyes. Then the other man's gaze met Garret's as though trying to read him. "Not tonight, babe." He disengaged his arm. "I haven't seen my sisters in weeks. I'll catch up with you tomorrow."

Chantelle smiled at him, but Garret could see the set to her jaw. "Or not." She flounced away from him, past Tori, and into the darkness beyond the reach of the deck lighting. A minute later a vehicle started then drove away.

Garret tore his gaze away from Tori toward her brother. "I think I'll call it a night, myself. If I may get my keys from inside."

James crossed his arms and widened his stance as he stared Garret down. "I don't think you can just walk away from that explosion."

"Who knew you were hiding a firecracker like that one?" Sawyer chuckled. "Didn't know you had it in you, Morrison."

Lauren rolled her eyes at Sawyer before turning back to Garret. "Why didn't you say something that day we were talking about her Spokane concert?"

"She's in my past. I didn't bring my past west with me." Then why had he dumped everything on Tori just a bit ago? Everything but Chantelle. That woman had dumped herself here.

"We don't *bring* our pasts," observed Cheri. "Our pasts helped make us who we are today. Trust me, mine has some ugly bits I wish I could pretend never happened."

Right. She'd run away from a wedding with Kade Delgado and become pregnant with Dillon Scarborough's child. But there had eventually been repentance and a Christmas reunion.

Kade slid his arm around his wife, rubbing her shoulder gently as she continued. "Whatever it is, God's got it, Garret. We give it to Him and then we trust Him to use it to shape our lives. I ran for six years, living in fear Dillon would find Harmony and me. Running didn't make the problem go away. In fact, it gave Dillon more power over me than he already had."

Kade nodded. "She's right, Morrison. Now that Scarborough has access to his daughter, he rarely takes it. For him, it was all about control. Now that we've forgiven him and offered to work with him within specific parameters, it's not worth his trouble."

Forgive Chantelle? Was that what they were asking

him to do? Garret shook his head, the verbal refusal on his lips. But what Chantelle had done to him had been nothing compared to what Dillon had done to Cheri and Cheri had done to Kade. Chantelle had only destroyed his career aspirations. The rest? He'd allowed the rest to happen in self-protection.

Garret looked around the group. His friends, all ready to do battle with him and for him, even though he hadn't shared everything with them. Then his gaze landed on the two young teens, eyes wide, mouths open. This wasn't the moment to get into the depths. "Is there any food? I'm starving."

"Men." That came from Denae. Just a comment, not an indictment.

Trevor kissed her cheek. "Nailed it."

Tori shepherded her charges toward the lighted gazebo, completely avoiding Garret's gaze.

He deserved that. She'd pitied him for the things he'd told her, but this? His stupidity in falling for Chantelle and revealing too much to someone so conniving wasn't pitiable. It was lousy judgment in the light of all the evidence he'd seen.

Adam stopped beside Garret. "Tell me more?"

Garret looked at the other man. "There's nothing much else to say. I'd forgive her if she showed any remorse, but you saw how she was about it. Like it was no big deal."

"You were supposed to be the keyboardist for that band?"

"All but signed."

"There are bigger things in store for you."

That was what the other guy got out of this? "Thanks." Maybe. "At least now you know what you're in for with her."

"We only met a few weeks ago when she sang the national anthem at the opening ceremony for one of the bigger rodeos. After I won the competition — beating out Sawyer Delgado, I might add — she approached me with those wide blue eyes of hers and told me how awesome I was." Adam scratched the back of his neck. "What guy doesn't like hearing that? I mean, you've got to admit it. She's pretty hot."

"Hot enough to burn a guy." Garret's gaze drifted over to Tori. She reached for something on the table, her back to him. Tori didn't have the Dolly Parton hair and curves Chantelle flaunted. She was beautiful in a more down-home way. Pretty. Sweet. Fun. A woman who'd tucked against him as perfectly as Jenna had done. Who kissed him as though she meant it.

Garret'd kissed her back until he heard Chantelle's unmistakable voice not fifty feet away. He'd recoiled in shock, and Tori had taken that as one more rejection. Of course, she had. If there was anything Garret was good at, it was blockading himself against Tori's charms.

She'd given him a dozen chances to redeem himself in the past few months. Either she'd give him one more, or he'd lost out forever. It would be his own fault if that happened.

TORI STUCK to her young charges like she was the

superglue holding them together. What was she supposed to do with the knowledge that Garret Morrison had once dated someone as famous as Chantelle Devereaux? Before the artist had become a big name, sure, but Garret might have become that celebrity.

She'd always thought of him as an all-around cowboy and talented small-town musician. She'd never once dreamed he composed music or could have played in a band she heard on the radio. Might have been the star in a band carrying his name.

Here she'd been certain she was the answer to his dreams. They'd settle down in Saddle Springs, maybe taking over Canyon Crossing Stables from his sweet elderly parents. Have a few babies — cousins for Meg's and James's kids — and just live a normal, everyday life as regular American citizens.

But Garret's dreams had once been much bigger and, now that he was facing his past, those dreams would resurge and call him again. He might not have been writing music for the past five years — though how would she know? — but he'd kept his skills up playing for the worship team. Why had it never crossed her mind to wonder why an ordinary guy would have an actual music room housing a grand piano in his house? Even Delgados or Cavanaghs didn't, though their houses were much larger.

Tori was so embarrassed. In all the reasons she'd told herself why Garret kept away from her, she hadn't considered that the big one was that she simply wasn't... enough. He had his sights set elsewhere. When his parents passed on, he'd go back to the future he'd once all but had in his grasp.

She forced her focus on Alexia beside her. "Enjoying the food?" To Tori, it all tasted like sawdust.

The girl licked her fingers, moaning. "We need to steal your chef. He's amazing."

"Agreed," added Emma. "This is far better than anything Maeve has ever made. My taste buds think they've died and gone to heaven."

That's how Tori's had felt while Garret returned her kiss. Intoxicated and alive like never before. How quickly things changed. More to the point, how quickly things slid back into their five-year rut.

Now he stood talking to Adam, probably about Chantelle and the world he'd inhabited with her, without so much as a glance Tori's direction. Not that she was staring at him. She'd only peeked a couple of times, so it was possible she'd missed it if he had. What an idiot she was.

After the two men loaded their plates, they joined James and Kade across the circle. The twins went back for seconds, and Sawyer usurped Alexia's spot.

He nudged her with his elbow. "Hey."

Tori sighed. "Haven't we said enough to each other?"

"I don't know. Have we? I didn't think Adam would know anyone here, but look at him."

"You brought him so you wouldn't feel weird around your big brothers."

"Well, yeah. I guess. You have to admit I'm not like them."

"They've grown up, and you haven't bothered."

"Really, Tori? You live with your parents. You're hardly one to talk."

She skewered him with a look. "There's more than one way to grow up. Being a responsible human being works for me. And I don't live with my parents. I have my own place."

"Do you think Garret and Chantelle will get back together?"

Her gut froze. "How should I know? It didn't sound like there was any love lost between them. Besides, isn't she dating Adam?"

Sawyer stretched his legs out in front of him. "I'm guessing he was supposed to hop up and leave with her when she wanted him to."

"Whatever. I don't care. I want to know if you're going to sneak your way into Anna's good graces again." She didn't care about that, either, but it should serve to divert the subject. "Though heaven knows what she saw in you to begin with."

He placed his hand over his heart and gave her a pouty puppy-dog look.

"Stuff it, Sawyer. You're not half as hot as you think you are."

He laughed. "And that's why I like you, Tori. You tell it like you see it."

"So long as you remember I'll never like you romantically."

"Suits me fine."

Tori slugged his arm. "You know how to take a girl down a peg."

"You did the same to me."

She had, at that, and couldn't stifle a laugh.

The twins settled on the ground near their big brother. Garret glanced toward Tori, his gaze flicking between her and Sawyer. As usual, nothing showed on his face. How could a guy kiss like he'd kissed her and then blank his expression this completely just minutes later?

Sawyer leaned closer. "Want a cupcake? I'll get you one."

"I don't think—"

"You don't need to watch your weight, you know." He waved his hands in an hourglass. "A cupcake won't hurt you any."

"That's not why." But did she really want to explain why her heart was heavy to Sawyer Delgado, of all people? Not a chance. "You know what? Thanks. I'd love one."

"That's my girl."

"Stop it. You know there's nothing between us. Never will be."

"You keep saying that." He'd been halfway off the bench but now turned toward her. "But I'm curious why."

"Let's start with Anna."

"Look, Anna and I went out a few times in June. She's pretty hot, if you know what I mean."

"I don't *want* to know what you mean."

"Go ahead. Keep your head in the sand. There were adult activities, if you must know. And now she's not returning my texts."

"Are you planning on marrying her?"

Sawyer shrugged. "Probably not. Why?"

"Then maybe you should save the adult activities for your wife."

"Too late, Mom."

"Look, Sawyer, I care about you." She set her hand on his arm and looked deeply in his eyes. "No clue why, but there you have it. And I don't know why you've tossed aside the way your parents raised you. Why you've decided God's not good enough for you, but He is. He's faithful. He's worthy. You think you're God's gift to women, some sort of macho cowboy, but we can see through that." Although, did Anna see through him? Maybe that's why she'd quit responding. "It's an act, Sawyer. Somewhere inside you, the kid who led youth group rallies ten years ago still resides. Why not dig him out, brush him off, and see what happened to him? He was a good guy. He was real."

The cocky look had left his eyes as he searched hers. "You don't understand."

"You're right. I don't, but I'm praying for you."

CHAPTER 21

How could she?

Less than an hour ago she'd tracked Garret down and kissed him. Okay, this time he'd started it, but she'd come to him, and she'd definitely kissed him back. She'd set his blood on fire from head to toe.

And now she was having a cozy one-on-one with Sawyer, laughing with him, touching him, pressing her arm against his, looking in his eyes. *Look, Sawyer, I care about you.*

Garret had been passing by to grab another round of cupcakes for Adam and the twins when he'd overheard. He hadn't hung around to hear the rest of her profession.

Was this just how she was? A player? How had he not noticed? No. This wasn't her.

Plate full of cupcakes, he glanced over again. Heard Sawyer's chuckle and saw Tori's genuine smile, the one that dimpled her cheek, before Sawyer sprang to his feet and turned to the dessert table. Garret pivoted away just before the younger man caught him staring. Whew.

Garret thrust the plate at Adam and turned to James. "Mind grabbing my keys? I think I'll call it a night."

James's gaze shifted past Garret. "It's not what it looks like." He pulled him off to one side, out of earshot of the Cavanaghs.

"What's not what?"

"Don't feign ignorance, Morrison. My sister isn't interested in Delgado."

"I need to check on my mom. I hate leaving them alone for this long."

James's face softened. "I'm sure it's a big worry. I remember when we weren't sure if my dad was going to make it or not. It was really tough."

"We know the outcome. We just don't know when."

"I'm sorry. I wasn't trying to be insensitive."

Garret let out a long breath. "I know. There's just been... a lot going on." Did that cover the situation with Tori as well? It would have to. "Some days I'm not sure which direction is up."

"Where God is."

He blinked. "Pardon me?"

"That's the direction that's up. Where God is. No matter what is happening, turn toward the light, and God will meet you."

"It's not as simple as it sounds."

James searched him with a look of compassion. "I know."

"Today's been a bit of a roller coaster what with Chantelle and all. And I need some space."

"If I hand over your keys, will you go fly fishing with me in the morning? I'd like to ride up the creek behind Canyon Crossing and get some trout. Also, I'd like you not to shut me out anymore. You can't do it all alone, man. That's what friends are for."

Like he was going to explain to his best friend that he was in love with his sister and she seemed to have moved on minutes after they'd kissed. He met James's gaze. "We can go fishing, but I can't promise to dump my load on you."

"You up for worship team? Because Lauren and I aren't really good at it without the piano."

Garret closed his eyes for a second. "Not yet. Not this week."

"Okay." Disappointment colored James's voice. "We'll keep praying for you and your folks."

"Thanks."

"And for you and my sister."

Garret took a step back as he stared at his friend.

James held up both hands in defense. "It's none of my business, but man, you need to get on the same page. You know why I've got the right to tell you that?"

"I doubt I want to know."

"Because you interfered big time when Lauren and I were doing the big avoidance thing. Looking back, knowing what I know now, and then looking at you and Tori...? Well, it's pretty obvious."

"And Sawyer?" As soon as the words escaped, Garret wished them back, but it was too late.

The glow from the gazebo lights caught the twinkle in James's eyes. "They've known each other since they were in diapers. They have an odd sort of relationship, but it's definitely not love."

"You and Lauren had an odd sort of relationship, too," Garret pointed out. "And you both denied it was love."

James chuckled. "You got me there, Morrison. But this is different. You guys said we were watching each other when we thought no one would notice. Definitely not the case with Sawyer and my sister." He leaned closer. "You and Tori, though? Totally that."

The kiss by the creek conceded James's assessment, but the moment seemed lost forever. All Garret could think was she wanted nothing to do with a guy who'd been so duped by the likes of Chantelle. And then Sawyer made his move, and she went for it.

Wasn't it just two months ago Garret had wished she'd fall for Sawyer instead? Who knew having his wish come true could be this painful?

He held out his hand. "My keys?"

"Sure you won't stay for fireworks? We can start lighting them off in just a couple of minutes. Let me check with Lauren."

"I've had rather enough fireworks, frankly." At least of the Chantelle variety. The Tori variety? He could use a whole lot more.

James chuckled. "Yeah, I can see that." He dipped into his shorts pocket and pulled out Garret's fob. "Here you go, Morrison. See you at sunrise."

And to think Garret could have wrestled those keys away from James any time he wanted. Without a backward glance, he strode up the drive toward his truck.

TORI POURED a tall glass of iced tea and slipped out to her quiet back deck facing the still water. The sliver of moon flirted with a few fluffy clouds overhead, gleaming on the small lake. A cricket or two chirped, and a bat swooped.

The fireworks were a memory. She'd sat alone on the beach near her brother's house amid the snuggling couples, her charges flanking their big brother. And then she'd paddled the twins back across the dark lake and sent them up to the loft.

She felt less alone on her deck than she had in the group. The reminder that she was the tagalong stuck. They were James's friends, and they let her hang out with them. Lauren claimed to want to be friends, but that was because she felt sorry for Tori. When she had girl-stuff to share, she went to Denae or Cheri. Maybe even Meg.

Garret had talked to James for a few minutes then headed out without a backward glance. To find Chantelle? That didn't feel right. Whatever had been between the two of them was long gone.

But what about what was between Tori and Garret? He was so hard to read. Those kisses by the creek... was she misremembering? Had it really happened, or was her overactive imagination striking again?

Tori touched her lips. They remembered. It felt real, but so was the way he'd cut her off, had brusque words with Chantelle, talked to the guys while they stuffed their faces, then left without another glance at Tori.

The vision of the voluptuous blonde stuck in her

mind. If that's the kind of woman Garret was used to having on his arm, no wonder he hadn't given her a second look for five years. She'd thought maybe a new cut and color and an updated wardrobe would make the difference. Yeah, right. Next to Nashville's sweetheart, Tori remained a country bumpkin.

Well, that's who she was. Nothing but a cowgirl. She wasn't even capable of keeping Emma and Alexia out of trouble. Their father terrified her with his brusque, no-nonsense demeanor, so different from Dad's gentle spirit. Bringing the twins here was just as much a mistake. They hadn't discovered Matt and Lionel yet, but when they did, Tori would have her hands full.

She'd jumped at Noah's offer much too quickly. She didn't have the training for the task she'd signed on for. It was only for a month, and that was half over. She'd survive, but Declan Cavanagh needed to find another solution long-term. If he even stopped to consider his youngest children at any point.

That wasn't Tori's problem. It couldn't be.

She drew her knees up to her chest and hugged them to herself as a light breeze picked up off the lake. It was so still. The guests in the nearby cabins had cheered the fireworks across the water and then, apparently, retired for the night.

Lord, are You out there?

She stared at the night sky as the slivered moon slid behind a thicker cloud. Pitch dark. Just like her spirits tonight.

Jesus, have I been too busy making my own plans to be open to

Your direction? Did I assume that the desires of my heart were the same as Yours?

It seemed that way. She'd let herself live in default mode, and the variations from it were few and far between. She'd fixated on Garret because... because why? He'd seemed safe. He wasn't safe. He had more baggage than a train of packhorses.

From Garret she'd ricocheted to Rockstead Ranch, but chaperoning two young teens under the sharp gaze of their domineering father and varied attention from their assorted brothers had been leaping from the frying pan into the fire.

But, she couldn't stay here forever, either. She couldn't bear watching Garret suffer through his mom's illness and then pack up and leave Saddle Springs for good.

Was becoming a teacher the right thing, after all? It had been her dream all through her childhood and teen years, until the world had tipped on its axis after her dad's accident.

A passionate, caring teacher made all the difference. She could do that in a school setting without living in for a family like the Cavanaghs. By the time she was certified, Garret would be long gone, and she could return to Saddle Springs. Maybe rent a place in town like the duplex Lauren used to own. She could come out to the Flying Horseshoe several times a week to ride Coaldust, hang out with her nieces and nephews, and visit her parents.

Why did that future look so gray and desolate? She'd get used to living without Garret.

Her fingers touched her mouth.

Could she give up that dream after those lip-searing kisses by the creek?

She had to. He'd deviated momentarily, but he'd snapped back behind his facade in no time flat at the reminder of what he'd lost years ago.

Tori was nothing compared to Chantelle and all Garret had left in Kentucky. She couldn't compete. Didn't want to. If she wasn't enough the way she was, then she wasn't enough.

I have loved you with an everlasting love.

That was the Lord speaking, not Garret. Jesus had covered her lack with His own forgiveness and abundance. She might not be enough for Garret, but she was enough for Jesus. He'd loved her, redeemed her, and given her purpose. She just needed to find it and embrace it.

Tori rose to her feet and crossed to the deck railing. Leaning on it, she peered into the dark night at the millions of pricks of starlight. One shot across the blackness in a blaze that disappeared without a trace in a bare instant.

The God who created the universe loved her. He had a plan for her and would not abandon her. Dad always told her you couldn't turn a parked vehicle. Sure, you could pretend by yanking on the steering wheel, but the car stayed pointing the way it had been before. If you actually wanted to change the direction, you had to put it in drive and apply pressure to the accelerator. Then a twist of the wheel made a difference, but not before.

She'd send in her application to the college in

Missoula for January's intake. That would be her foot on the gas with much prayer for guidance.

They might not accept her. But they might.

Either way, she'd pray the result was God's direction in her life.

CHAPTER 22

G arret met James at the corral as the first rays of sunlight crept across the stables. He'd saddled Trudy and Boomerang and strapped his fly rod case across his back. James stuffed containers of food into his saddlebags and mounted up, saluting Garret with his travel coffee mug.

Words were unnecessary. No more a morning person than Garret was, his friend was willing to enjoy the silence and stillness of dawn. Good thing, since sleep had been all but absent throughout the night as the evening replayed on endless loops in his mind.

They still repeated.

Tori's sweet kisses. The ugly reality of Chantelle blasting into Garret's current world. Tori avoiding looking at him, but comfortable with Sawyer. And then back to her kisses at the creek.

Why couldn't God have kept Chantelle's world from ever intersecting Garret's again? The timing was incredibly horrific.

"Dude." James nudged Boomerang up beside Trudy. "Talk."

Garret shook his head.

James's sigh was loud enough to be heard over the creaking leather and plodding hooves.

"It's not that easy."

"Who said anything about easy? I'm as private as the next guy. You know that. But every once in a while, a man needs someone to talk to. You're the guy who needs to talk. I'm the guy God sent to listen."

Garret angled a glance at his friend. Had God really sent James? Certainly keeping everything close to the vest hadn't done Garret any favors. But still, James was the brother of the woman Garret loved.

Yes, loved.

His barricade had cracked just a little last night, and the light that had seeped through that gap had revealed the truth he'd been hiding from.

"I think there's more to your life story than the bit Chantelle mentioned."

"There is." Of course, there was. He was thirty years old. He'd lived a quarter of a century before ever meeting the man he now called friend. Garret winced inwardly. How could he consider James his friend if he blocked everything away? He'd told Tori and not sworn her to secrecy. Who knew if she'd told anyone? And what did it matter? She hadn't run screaming at the revelations.

Maybe James wouldn't, either. And if he did, would Garret be any worse off?

"I'm adopted," he blurted out. "My birth mom died of a drug overdose. No one found us for three days."

"I'm sorry," James said simply, eyes full of compassion.

"Tuck and Nancy took me in as a foster kid and then adopted me."

"God was looking after you."

That's what Tori had said. What his new parents had told him, too. What he'd believed himself for many, many years. Still did, buried deep beneath the other layers of hurt.

"I was married. My... wife..." His voice broke on the word. "My wife died in a crash on our way to the honeymoon hotel."

"I'm so sorry."

"And then I met Chantelle two years later."

"And then you moved west."

Garret nodded.

"That's a lot."

"Tell me."

"I've been reading the Psalms lately." James dug into his hip pocket and pulled out his phone. He thumbed it on, poked around a bit, then glanced over. "Psalm 66 was this morning."

"Oh?" For all the passages and verses Garret had memorized as a child, this chapter didn't ring a bell.

"Starting here in verse eight. 'Bless our God, O peoples; let the sound of his praise be heard, who has kept our soul among the living and has not let our feet slip. For you, O God, have tested us; you have tried us as silver is tried. You brought us into the net; you laid a crushing burden on our backs; you let men ride over our heads; we went through fire and through water'..." James looked up. "Sound about right?"

Garret took a deep breath and nodded. Crushing burdens, being trampled, fire, water... yeah. All of that.

James looked back at his phone. "'We went through fire and through water; yet you have brought us out to a place of abundance.'" He tapped the device and shoved it back in his pocket.

A place of abundance? That's what Dad had said, too. Garret knew that one. *The thief comes only to steal and kill and destroy. I came that they may have life and have it abundantly.*

"John 10:10."

Garret gave James a startled look. He must have recited it out loud.

"So here's the question, Garret. Are you going to let the thief steal, kill, and destroy? Are you going to wallow in the crushing burden and the fire and water? Or are you going to move through and claim the abundance?"

He wanted to take offense at the word wallow, but wasn't that what he'd been doing? In himself, he claimed no one needed to know the sordid details of his past. He'd come to Montana to reinvent himself as a man who held himself aloof so he wouldn't get hurt again.

Guess what?

He was hurt. And this time it was his own fault.

Was Tori part of the abundant life Jesus wanted to shower on him? Maybe. But, even if she wasn't — or he'd irrevocably ruined everything — God was bigger than that.

"That's a lot to take in, Carmichael. Thanks."

James studied him for a long moment then nodded. "What's a good fly the trout are hitting on these days? Lauren says if I'm not bringing in the bacon today, the least I can do is provide fish for supper."

Garret cracked a grin. "Parachute Adams. Is there any other fly?"

"I'll put my Elk Hair Caddis against your Adams any day of the week."

"You're on."

"My father needs you to bring the twins home."

Tori clenched the phone tighter in her hand at Noah's words. "But we've only been gone twenty-four hours."

"I know." Noah's voice softened. "But when my mother figured out they were gone, she kind of lost it."

"But..." The girls had kissed their mother goodbye. She'd even waved from the window. "Noah, this can't work. How am I supposed to do what I'm hired for if they change their minds on a whim?" Oh, no. She should definitely not be badmouthing Noah's parents to anyone, let alone him.

"I get it." He sighed. "I thought you distracting them from the tension around here could only be a good thing. It's like the twins are pawns in a chess game between Declan and my mother, neither of whom are thinking rationally."

That was the first time he'd called his stepdad by his first name in Tori's hearing, showcasing the frustration in his voice. How had Noah turned out to be one of the good ones in a dysfunctional family like that?

On the other hand, everything had changed between her and Garret last night. Had changed twice. Sticking around the Flying Horseshoe wondering if or when he'd face up to what he'd done didn't sound appealing. And she'd rather not have a front row seat to his indecision.

Footsteps pounded on the log steps between Tori and the lake. "I get first dibs. I saw him first."

Tori covered the receiver. "Saw who first?" She could guess, though. The loft window looked out over the stable yard.

Alexia's eyes widened when she glanced over and saw Tori. "Umm… I didn't mean that the way it sounded."

Emma shoved her. "You totally did."

"Noah?" Tori said into the phone. "You're right. It was probably bad timing to bring them here. So, yes, we'll pack up and head back to Rockstead today."

Emma glared at her twin. "Now you've done it."

"It's not my fault."

"Nothing ever is."

"Exactly. It's totally yours."

"Girls." Tori tapped to end the call and set the phone down. "Your parents need you at home."

Alexia's hands found her hips. "I don't want to."

"We're not being given an option, honestly. I don't want to, either." Or she hadn't until overhearing their rivalry. "But those are the orders we've been given."

"Dad's just proving he's boss." Alexia sighed.

Emma turned to Tori with a worried frown. "Is Mom okay?"

Define *okay*? "I'm not sure. Noah didn't say." Not in so many words. "So, instead of going horseback riding this morning, you need to go back up to the loft and pack your stuff. We need to be on the road in an hour."

"An hour?" Alexia curled her lip. "That's not even reasonable. Where's Adam? He can set things straight."

Emma nodded. "Yeah, where's Adam?"

"You're my responsibility, not your brother's." Tori pointed up the staircase. "So please just march back up there and start packing. I need to do the same."

Alexia muttered something rude under her breath and flounced up the steps. Emma held back a bit, searching Tori's face. Then she trailed her sister.

Tori tapped her mom's number on the cell phone as she entered her own bedroom and yanked her luggage out from under the bed. "Mom? There's been a change of plans." Again.

A FEW HOURS of fishing with a buddy had been just what Garret needed. After delivering his brief sermon and noting it had sunk in, James had changed the subject. They'd spoken of random, everyday things between reeling in several nice brookies each. They'd stopped by the miner's cabin and eaten their lunch in the shade. He'd even told James how much he loved that place, how he'd cleaned it out and hauled a decent mattress up here years ago. It had been his getaway when memories threatened to drag him under. A place where God met him.

Now they rounded a bend in the trail overlooking the

town of Saddle Springs, and James's phone began to ping with incoming texts.

This was as far into the back country as cell service reached. "Popular guy," Garret commented.

James thumbed the device on, and his brow furrowed as he read his messages. "It's Tori," he said tersely, reining Newton to a stop.

And here Garret had been congratulating himself that he hadn't dumped the tale of his lovesickness on his best friend. Now, he almost wished he had. "What's up?" Hopefully he'd kept his voice casual.

James scrolled, glanced at his watch, then scrolled some more. "A couple of hours ago, she texted and asked me to come load her car. Then she said she had to take the twins back to Rockstead." Scroll. "Then she said never mind, she'd get everything herself, that she didn't want to ask Matt to help." James looked up. "I wonder why not? He's capable of slinging backpacks and suitcases."

Garret managed a nonchalant shrug even as his gut squeezed. Tori was leaving again? Maybe had already left? While he dithered and caught fish, something was going on that he should have been aware of.

"Last text was twenty minutes ago, saying she'd see me in two weeks." He frowned and skewered Garret with a hard look. "I thought I'd said everything I needed to say to you, but now I'm not so sure. What happened last night, Morrison? Besides Chantelle."

Garret took a deep breath. "It's confusing."

His friend's eyebrows disappeared under the brim of his cowboy hat. "You think?"

"I'm in love with your sister. I tried not to be, but it happened anyway."

"Hallelujah," James muttered.

That didn't sound much like praise. "I'm sorry. Maybe it's best she's gone. I'll back off."

"Are you always this dense, or is this a special occasion?"

"P-Pardon me?"

"She's been in love with you for years. Does she even know you feel the same, or is that one more thing you've been bottling up and refusing to acknowledge? Honestly, man. You're like Aiden. My nephew refuses to let his peas touch his meat, and neither can touch his potatoes. Serve that kid stew? Not on your life. He compartmentalizes everything." James glared at Garret. "As do you."

"I didn't want to drag her down with my issues."

"The issues we've already agreed God's dealt with so that you can step into His abundant life. Those issues, like actually forgiving Chantelle?"

Garret nodded, looking down at his hands clenching Trudy's reins.

"Okay, so last night. What happened last night? You only came to our party because you thought Tori was away. Right?"

"Yes. The last time we'd seen each other she'd dropped off food for the meal train. She, uh, kissed me."

James rolled his eyes.

Garret narrowed his. "She did."

"Not disputing that. And I gather you pushed her away like you did at the wedding."

Everyone in town had likely noticed that and speculated on it.

"So. Last night."

"Not my finest hour." Although, there for a bit, it definitely had been. "We talked. I told her about my birth mom and about Jenna. We... kissed."

"As in, it was mutual this time." James wasn't exactly asking.

Garret nodded. Talk about an awkward discussion. "And then I heard Chantelle's voice."

"And panicked."

"Yeah. So now Tori's not talking to me again."

"Did you *try*, man? Seriously. Because what I remember is her hanging out with the twins and you talking to me and Adam. And then you leaving."

"That about covers it."

"Dude. Would you two talk to each other? Can you just, you know, open up a little? It's not going to kill you."

It felt like it might. "She didn't even look at me again."

James reached across the gap and thwacked Garret's arm. "You're blind, deaf, and stupid. I'm not sure I even want you for a brother-in-law. You've got to treat my sister better than this, Morrison."

"She probably doesn't want anything to do with me after Chantelle."

"This is the only time I'm going to say this, so listen up. Do you love my sister? Because, if you do, go find her. Talk to her. Make sure she knows. And once you're communicating? Stop overthinking things and ask her what she's thinking! Then listen and respond. Jeepers."

"Go find her?"

"Yeah. Go find her. You know what she's driving. You know there's only one highway between Saddle Springs and Rockstead."

Garret stared at James. "That wouldn't be... creepy?" But in his mind's eye, he could see her RAV4 ahead of him on the highway. He could see himself passing her and waving frantically for her to pull over. Then he'd wrench open her door, pull her out, and kiss her until they both gasped for air. He'd talk after that. Kissing first, talking second.

James angled a glare at him. "Creepy? What kind of word is creepy? I feel like I'm babysitting here."

"I'll do it."

CHAPTER 23

Tori pulled to a stop in front of the Cavanaghs' massive log-and-rock ranch house. "We're here." Not that the twins couldn't see that for themselves.

"I wanted to stay at the Flying Horseshoe longer," Alexia grumbled. "I never even got to talk to that cute guy."

Tori, on the other hand, was kind of done. The girls had both absolutely refused to tote their belongings to the SUV. They'd sat and watched her haul every single piece of their luggage down the log stairs and out to the car, and she'd had to grab a few grocery bags to stuff the last few items into since they'd packed so haphazardly.

Emma shoved her door open, bending to greet the dog that trotted over. "We never get what we want, anyway. So what's new?"

Tori wished she could clunk their heads together to see the blessings in their life. Sure, their family might not be perfect, but they had big brothers who cared about them and nearly anything they wanted, so long as it was at Rockstead. She had a sinking feeling they were going to test that last bit quite a lot as they grew older.

Across the yard, a man vaulted the corral fence and strode over, another pup at his heels. Declan. He was as fit as his sons, and the sight of it made Tori's heart hurt. Why had her own father's legs been mangled in that freak accident?

Declan stopped a few feet away, piercing eyes taking them in from beneath the brim of his well-worn felt cowboy hat. His feet were braced, and his thumbs hooked through belt loops. "You're back."

Emma's back straightened almost imperceptibly, and Tori realized hers was doing the same. Across the vehicle, Alexia emerged. "Hi, Dad."

He nodded at her.

Where was the running into their daddy's arms, the big hugs and twirls that Tori's dad had lavished on her when she was their age? Forget wishing Bill Carmichael had retained his mobility. He'd kept his faith and his gentle, loving spirit, something Declan Cavanagh didn't seem to ever have had.

Declan pointed to the house. "Your mother wants to see you."

The twins scampered off as though relieved to be released from their father's domineering presence.

"I'll get one of the boys to come unload your car."

"Thank you, sir."

He nodded, still watching her.

Tori shifted from one foot to the other then took a

deep breath and lifted her chin. "I'm not sure what you want from me now? I hired on for a month and..."

"Exactly. That hasn't changed."

So she was back at Rockstead for the next two weeks. Okay, then. "Thank you, sir."

He turned, stuck his fingers in his mouth, and gave a piercing whistle. The youngest Cavanagh brother jogged over from the barn. "Yes, sir?"

"Take Miss Carmichael's things to her room. And your sisters' bags to theirs."

"You got it, sir." Ryder saluted his father and grinned at Tori. "Good to see you again."

For all the world like she'd been gone for a month instead of a couple of days. "You, too." He was a good kid.

Tori reached into the RAV4 for her purse then heard another vehicle coming up the drive. She turned to look, not that it mattered to her which brother was arriving. Anyone driving in to the remote ranch was a novelty, though, as she'd discovered in her previous visit. Okay. Two more weeks. She could do this. Declan was paying her handsomely to chaperone his daughters.

A red pickup rumbled around the final curve with a plume of dust, and Tori's heart all but seized. She knew that truck. Garret. He couldn't be here. But he was. Why? Her feet riveted to the gravel parking lot even as her fingers covered her mouth. Those kisses last night — was he having as much trouble brushing them aside as she was?

Garret hit the brakes in a cloud of dust and leaped

out of the cab before the engine cut out. He rounded the truck, gaze fixed on hers. "Tori."

Garret was here, and his face revealed an openness she hadn't seen in a long time.

"Who are you?" Declan stepped between them, chest out. "Didn't you see the *slow* signs? See all that dust you stirred up? Have a little respect."

"I'm Garret Morrison. And you are?"

"Declan Cavanagh, owner of Rockstead." The blustery man waved his hand to encompass the huge ranch.

"Sorry about the dust." Garret stepped around Declan, but the man blocked him.

"What do you want here?"

Garret looked past the big man's shoulder. "I came to tell Tori I love her."

The ranch whirled around Tori as she stared into Garret's eyes from several feet away. Had she heard him correctly? Could she trust him, when he'd backed off before after making his attraction clear? But the tortured look was gone.

An elbow nudged Tori's arm. "Is he a good guy? Because I'm pretty sure I could take him out if you want him gone."

Tori blinked and turned to Ryder. "He's a good guy. I think... I think I might be in love with him, too."

Declan snorted. "All that kind of mush makes a man weak."

"On the contrary." Garret squared his shoulders as he faced the big man. "It takes a strong man to admit he needs love. That he's been stuck in the past far too long and it's time to leave it behind and reach for the abundant life God has planned for him."

"And now you're bringing God into it." Declan rolled his eyes. "Look, you can talk to her for half an hour, but she's my employee, and that's all I give you. And only if she wants to talk to you." He turned and raised his eyebrows at Tori.

"Yes, please."

He checked his watch and turned to Ryder. "Quit gawking, boy. Get the Toyota unloaded."

"Yes, sir." Ryder winked at Tori then popped open the hatch.

Tori took two steps toward Garret as he moved toward her. "Do you mean that?" she breathed.

"I absolutely do." He clasped both her hands in his, searching her face. "I love you."

She'd spent five years waiting for this moment. Waiting to hear this profession. Waiting to see tenderness shine from his eyes as he looked at her. "I love you, too."

"Can you ever forgive me for being such a dunce?"

She tried to pull her hands free so she could wrap her arms around him, but his grip was ironclad. So she stretched to her tiptoes and brushed a kiss across his lips, igniting an exploding fire that blasted through her whole body. "Forgiven. Just don't do it again."

Declan cleared his throat sharply.

Tori's face flamed from more than the kiss. She pulled Garret beside her and started walking toward Kathryn's gardens. A little privacy for what remained of their half hour would not go amiss.

GARRET PUSHED ASIDE the niggling doubt that this wasn't real. But the fragrance of riotous flowers filled the heated summer air. A horse whinnied, blocking the buzz of honeybees for a brief instant. Most of all, Tori's fingers twined with his as she led him toward a bench beside a little waterfall cascading into a pond. Bushes and taller trees cocooned the bench from the vast back deck of the ranch house.

"Tori." He turned toward her, and his free hand brushed the side of her cheek. "Are you sure? Because I've been an idiot." Or, as James had put it, blind, deaf, and stupid.

"Tell me what happened?" Those hazel eyes with glints of green and brown and gold looked into his.

"I told you a bit the other night." Had it only been yesterday? "I've been afraid, as though denying I had feelings would mean nothing could hurt me." He closed his eyes for a second. "I was a captive to my fears instead of trusting God to lead me. It's all so obvious now, but it seemed to make sense at the time."

He placed his palms around her face, reveling in the smooth skin beneath his thumbs, the way his fingers tangled in her short hair. "You're so beautiful."

Tori's hands slid around his hips then shifted to his shoulder blades. "You're amazing."

"I'm not. You know I'm not. You know I'm—"

"Garret." Her whisper brushed against his chin.

He didn't deserve this. And, one day, she'd see he

wasn't worth the trouble. Having faced his fears once didn't mean they were vanquished forever.

"Garret, I know you're not perfect, but that doesn't keep you from being amazing. It doesn't keep you from being the man I love. We're human. We make mistakes, but God..."

But God. Wasn't that the truth? "'But God, being rich in mercy, because of the great love with which he loved us, even when we were dead in our trespasses, made us alive together with Christ.'"

At her raised eyebrows, he added, "Ephesians 4:5-6."

"I think there's more to that section."

"There is. My dad had me memorize it when I was a kid. Verse seven goes on to say, 'so that in the coming ages he might show us the immeasurable riches of his grace in kindness toward us in Christ Jesus.'"

"Do you think that only means in the distant future?"

Garret winced but held his gaze steady on her trusting eyes. "I lived like it was, but I've been reminded several times lately of John 10:10: 'The thief comes only to steal and kill and destroy. I came that they may have life and have it abundantly.' I've been listening to the thief of joy, but I'm done with that, Tori. I am stepping into the abundant life God has promised."

Did she know what that meant to him? More than spiritual, though definitely that, too. He traced her cheekbones with his thumbs, marveling at the acceptance and love shining on her face. "I want to be worthy of your love, Tori."

"You already are. You're a child of the one true King, remember?"

"I had Matthew West on repeat on the trip over here. That song is like my testimony. *Hello, my name is regret...*" He took a deep breath, shaking his head.

"Not anymore, Garret." Her fingers slid into his hair at the back of his neck. "Your name isn't defeat, either. You've been saved, you've been changed, and you've been set free."

He absorbed her words, the words of the song. The shackles on his heart released just a little more. "Adoption is a beautiful thing. What my parents did for me... it's just a small picture of what God did for any of us who crave a new beginning."

"They rescued you, cared for you, loved you."

"They did. Not just Kellen and me — that's my older brother — but countless foster kids who came through our home. They'd have adopted everyone if they could have. It crushed them when their kids were returned to situations where they weren't loved or safe, but they kept on loving. Kept on opening their home."

How could he not have seen how opposite his own reactions to life had been? He'd been taught openness and loving without expectation of anything in return, but that's not how he'd lived. It's not how he'd treated Tori.

"They're wonderful people, Garret. I feel so bad. I ran into your mom at Shear Inspirations a few weeks ago. She wanted to go for coffee, but I brushed her off. I was too busy."

He caressed her lips. "She'd love to have you stop by. She's been praying for you. For us."

"She's a treasure. Is she... is she going to be okay?"

The truth stabbed at him, and he reeled slightly.. "We've been praying for a miracle, of course, but it doesn't look like God is providing one. The cancer — it's everywhere. The doctors don't expect her to make it to Christmas."

"I'm so sorry."

"Don't be." His response surprised himself. "She's ready to go. She's lived for Jesus for many years, and she's ready to meet Him face-to-face."

"Will you be okay?"

That was a loaded question. "Not gonna lie, it's going to be really tough. It already is. But Dad is a tower of strength for her and for me, and they're still memorizing scripture together."

Tori swallowed hard, tears welling in her eyes. "That's beautiful."

"It kind of is." His voice choked up. "'Let not your hearts be troubled. Believe in God; believe also in me. In my Father's house are many rooms. If it were not so, would I have told you that I go to prepare a place for you?'"

"John fourteen," she whispered.

Garret nodded and cleared his throat to continue. "'And if I go and prepare a place for you, I will come again and will take you to myself, that where I am you may be also. And you know the way to where I am going.'"

"They've given you a precious heritage, Garret."

"They really have. I've been blind to that at times, but now, I want to savor every moment." He kissed her to show her one of the things he was delighting in. "She only has one real regret." Oh, no. This was far too early for this particular confession.

"What's that?" Tori leaned back and looked up at him innocently, her fingers toying with the lapels of his snap-front shirt.

He took a deep breath and raised his eyebrows. "She wanted to see me married. Settled into my future."

"Is that right?" A grin twitched the corners of Tori's mouth as she peeked up at him.

What was it she'd said last night? More kissing. Less talking. Because that particular conversation needed a little more planning.

"That's right." And he kissed her.

CHAPTER 24

Tori set two cups of tea on the small table in Mrs. Morrison's studio. The room was taking on the look and smell of a sickroom. "I'm so sorry I blew you off that day in Shear Inspirations. I was afraid to talk to you." She gave the older woman an awkward smile. Other than all that time in the hospital after Dad's accident, she hadn't been around many sick people, and that had been totally different.

"I understand, my dear." Garret's mom tugged her fleece throw tighter around her legs and reached for the peach tea. "And I'll admit I was interfering, or trying to. I didn't need to do that. God was looking after my sweet boy all along. I just needed to keep trusting Him."

"Trusting is hard," Tori admitted. She curled her legs up under her in the other easy chair and took a sip of the tea. If Nancy Morrison was looking for a prim and proper lady for her son, she should have never moved her family to Saddle Springs.

"Jesus never lets us down."

Tori searched her serene face. How could she have such faith even while facing end-stage cancer?

"I have so many things to be thankful for, sweet girl. When Tucker and I couldn't conceive, God sent us dozens of children who needed a safe place to land, if even for only a short time. Our Kentucky ranch was the perfect antidote to the inner city so many came from." She smiled, lost in thought. "We were able to provide an oasis and share Jesus' love. Some of those children got in touch years later to let us know they'd found their way."

"Working with kids is a privilege. I didn't know what hit me with the Cavanagh twins, though. I'm sure you struggled with some of your foster kids."

"Tucker and I took some classes through a Christian university. That was a big help. But yes, many times all we could do was plead with our Heavenly Father for wisdom in guiding these precious young ones."

So many would rise up and call Nancy Morrison blessed. "That's why I want to become a teacher. I want to touch the lives of kids. Inspire them. Challenge them. But I know I need training to do it well. If I learned nothing else from Emma and Alexia, it's that."

The older woman nodded, a soft smile on her lips. "We can love with no training at all... just let the love of Jesus flow through us like a conduit. But for the other parts of those sensitive little hearts, training is very useful. You'll be a good teacher, my dear."

Tori's heart swelled at her calm assertion. Confirmation from a person she was coming to admire deeply. And Garret wanted her to follow her dream, too, though there was so much up in the air right now, she'd decided to try for fall enrollment rather than January.

What would their future look like? How long would his mom be part of it? Maybe not long, but her influence would remain forever.

She swallowed hard. "Garret said he has a brother?"

Mrs. Morrison bit her lip. "Kellen. We gave him everything he needed, same as the others. Same as Garret. But we haven't seen him in over fifteen years now." She met Tori's gaze, sorrow lining her eyes. "It's hard. You know you cannot save every one, but you want to. You do your best."

"We plant seeds. We water," Tori said softly. "But God gives the increase."

"First Corinthians 3:6-7. And this is why we are so delighted our son has found a treasure in you. You know the Lord. You know your Bible. I'm hoping — praying — God will give you many beautiful years together."

Tori felt her face flush, even though she was praying the same thing. It felt so strange to actually be acknowledged as a couple since her return from Rockstead a few days ago. The two weeks of texting and phone calls had given way to spending every evening together, often with their friends or families.

They'd visited Carmen and Spencer, and Tori had cradled their newborn in her arms, remembering what James had said about falling for baby Sophia two years ago. She felt the same with Jackson, an overwhelming longing to hold her own baby — Garret's baby — close to her breast. The sight of Garret holding Jackson had done a number on her heart, especially when he'd caught her watching and a deep look of understanding passed between them.

Sometimes Tori needed to pinch herself to remember this was all real. Garret loved her. The placid mask had disappeared and his own emotions rolled across his face. It helped that Pastor Roland had been counseling him regularly, and they planned to keep meeting together for a long time to come. Tori would join those sessions from time to time, but not yet, though Garret told her all about it. He told her he'd forgiven Chantelle. That he was thankful, even, for the circumstances that had sent him west. West to Tori.

Imagine. Garret talking about his feelings. Admitting he had some. That was the true miracle.

"Tell me all about Garret's childhood. Everything."

GARRET SWUNG his leg over Domi's back and slid to the ground, reaching for Tori as she dismounted Coaldust. The meadows above the Flying Horseshoe yellowed in the lazy heat of late August, but there was a little relief in the shadows of the pine forest.

They looped their reins loosely on the old fence, allowing the geldings room to graze in shade or sun and turned to each other without a spoken word. Just pulling Tori close made Garret's heart feel like he'd stepped into this scene from the depths of a Montana blizzard. So much cold. So many storms. So much blustering wind... and now peace. Warmth.

"I don't know how I thought I could live without

you." He pressed a kiss to her lips. "Thank you for being patient."

She laughed, her breath a soft caress across his cheek. "It wasn't easy, and I wasn't very patient."

"Five years, my love. That's patience."

"I didn't love you for five years. Only maybe four and a half."

He groaned and kissed her again, deeper this time. He had so much time to make up for. "Thank you for visiting my mom. You brighten her days." Like she brightened his.

"She's sweet. And she tells me so many stories of a little boy I wish I'd known."

"Just as well you didn't." Garret ran his thumbs down her cheeks. "But I want you to know it means a lot to her."

"I know." She looked about to say more, but shifted her gaze from his.

This was his moment. It was still too soon. Way too soon, by most standards. But he'd been a fool for five years... or maybe only four and a half. Either way, so long that his precious mother was dying before he'd come around.

"Tori?" He nuzzled her temple.

Her hands cradled his back as she turned to look at him. "Yes?"

For a second he forgot what he was going to say, and kissed her instead. "I love you."

She grinned, and he traced that little dimple on her cheek. "I know. And I'm thankful."

"I want to marry you."

Her smile faded as her eyes searched his. "I want to marry you, too."

His heart surged. "I've been thinking... please tell me what you think of my idea. I know it's unorthodox, but I guess I'm not ordinary, and circumstances really aren't, either."

"Tell me," she whispered.

"I know not everyone is engaged for a whole year like Trevor and Denae were, but most seem to be for at least a few months. And then there's this big church wedding."

Tori nodded.

"My mom... she doesn't have months from what the doctors say. At least not multiple good months. She's been doing well, all things considered, but—" he swallowed hard "—it's not going to last."

Garret dared to look at Tori. She patiently waited for him to get it all out. "I was wondering if you'd be willing to marry me at Canyon Crossing. Soon, with just our parents as witnesses. I want my mom to be there. To be well enough to appreciate it and celebrate with us." Celebrating might be the wrong word. It wasn't like she'd be dancing.

"Yes."

"I talked to your dad yester — wait. Did you say yes?"

She nodded, those hazel eyes glistening with unshed tears. "Yes."

He kissed her then, marveling at the trust she showed in him. He, who'd been so unworthy and hurt her so many times.

"We could maybe have a second ceremony?" she asked. "Our friends could join us out in the arena afterward. It doesn't have to be in the church. It doesn't have to be fancy, but I know they'll want to celebrate with us. It can be a potluck even. Denae and Cheri would have a ton of fun decorating the arena."

Now there was a plan. It would take longer to get his bride to himself, but it was a good compromise. "Good idea. If my mom is up to it, Dad could even wheel her out there for a bit."

Tori's face brightened. "She'd like that. I know she would."

This woman. She was so thoughtful, helping him make their wedding day into a special occasion for his mother. Not every bride would do that. Jenna would have, though. In his mind, he kissed her goodbye, vowing to remember the good times and not the horrific end.

Still, the thought of driving to their honeymoon hotel after the wedding shafted him with arrows of fear. He wouldn't let them take root, though. And maybe, just maybe, there was a way around that.

Two weeks later, on a sunny September Saturday, Tori stood in what would become her and Garret's bedroom at Canyon Crossing. This day had suddenly come upon them... and yet, not so suddenly. It had been five years in the making.

"You're beautiful." Voice choking, Mom smoothed Tori's hair and straightened her borrowed veil. "My baby girl."

"Ready for round one?" Pastor Roland peeked around the open door.

Tori beamed at him. "So ready."

"I'm proud of you, princess." Dad tucked her hand through the crook of his arm while Mom took his other arm. It was a question of who was holding up whom, but she was so blessed to have her daddy here to give her away.

The three of them made their way into Mrs. Morrison's studio, now her sickroom. Her body might be wasting away, but her eyes were bright. Her husband sat beside her, his arm around her shoulders, his other hand covering hers.

Tori's throat constricted and tears filled her eyes. If she and Garret could have half the love his parents had, their lives would be rich indeed.

She met the gaze of her beloved. He stood tall at his mom's bedside, his hands clasped behind his black tux. Tori's breath caught. He looked amazing, and the love that shone from his eyes filled her heart.

"Who gives this woman to be married to this man?" asked Pastor Roland.

"Her mother and I do." Dad searched her face with gentle eyes then he turned to face Garret. "Take care of her, son. She's a precious gift."

"I know it, sir. I will. I promise."

Mrs. Morrison pressed a tissue to her eyes as Tori leaned by her bedside and tucked her bouquet of flowers into a vase on the side table. "For you. Thank you for raising your son to honor the Lord."

Her thin hand pressed over Tori's. "We've prayed for you for more than twenty-five years," she whispered.

"Thank you." Tori wanted to say more, but she'd said it all in brief visits over the past few weeks. This was a moment for celebrating, not lingering in the past. Not for grieving what was coming.

She turned to Garret and took both his hands in hers, carefully angling so that their four parents all had a good view of their faces.

"We are gathered here today to witness and celebrate the union of Victoria June Carmichael and Garret Steven Morrison in holy matrimony."

Tori had never been more sure of anything in her life. To this man, she'd pledge herself gladly.

GARRET BENT and kissed his mother's soft cheek. She blinked at him with a gentle smile and drifted back asleep. But she'd witnessed the ceremony. She knew Tori was now his wife.

Wife.

Whoever would have thought?

Dad rose and gave Garret a swift hug. "'He who finds a wife finds a good thing and obtains favor from the Lord.'"

Garret blinked back emotion. "Proverbs 18:22. Thank you, Dad. You and Mom not only gave me a family, but you loved me and taught me every day." He laughed, but his throat clogged. "You were so patient with me. I owe you everything."

"You're mixing me up with your Heavenly Father, son. Now get going. There's another wedding with your name on it."

He glanced up at the clock. Cars and trucks already lined the driveway as their friends and neighbors gathered to witness their vows, though his father and Tori's mother had signed the legal documents as their witnesses. Now he waited for a text from James to say he and Lauren were back from setting up the trapper's cabin for the wedding night. Some couples might have to worry about allowing their friends access for fear of a short-sheeted bed or other pranks, but James knew Garret's history. He could be trusted.

Garret marveled to think he was married to Tori. He tugged her closer to his side, where she nestled against him. They'd make their home at Canyon Crossing for now. They'd be here for Mom's passing and Dad's initial adjustment at the least, allowing time for a decision on whether to sell the riding stables or keep them.

The thought that his mom would not be around to meet her grandchildren still hurt. It probably always would, but today he was stepping into his future.

His phone chimed with an incoming text. James and Lauren were back. Everyone was waiting. "Ready for another wedding, Mrs. Morrison?" he asked lightly.

Tori wrinkled her nose at him. "Must we?"

He laughed. "I think we must. It was your idea to do the whole thing twice, after all."

With one more quick clasp of his dad's hand, Garret slid his arm around his wife and led her from the room. "Quick stop in the music room? I've got a song for you."

"Oh? I want to hear it."

He settled in front of the grand piano, flipping the tails of his tux like he used to do when he was performing... a lifetime ago. His fingers found the melody, but Garret focused his gaze on his bride. "Hazel eyes with glints of green and brown and gold. Gazing into the windows of your soul. Everything you think is mirrored there — I'm powerless against you. I'm drowning in you..."

And his wife dabbed a tissue to those beautiful eyes.

ACKNOWLEDGMENTS

If you've read previous stories of mine, you'll know that cowboy romance is a minor variation on my usual themes of farm-and-garden such as in my flagship Farm Fresh Romance series. The Montana Ranches overlap slightly with both the Garden Grown Romances (part of the multi-author Arcadia Valley Romance series) where Cheri (Mackenzie) Delgado played a small role, and with the Urban Farm Fresh Romance series, where Denae Archibald appears as a friend to Sadie Guthrie in *Raindrops on Radishes*.

Thanks to Elizabeth Maddrey for being Chief Prodder and First Reader as well as a terrific author whose stories I enjoy reading!

I also appreciate my beta readers: Amy, Paula, and Gretchen. Thanks for loving this new direction, encouraging me, and catching my errors... although I'm sure I managed to leave a few in, even after my fabulous editor, Nicole, had her input. Thanks for sticking with me through all these years and stories, Nicole.

I'm also grateful for the Christian Indie Authors Facebook group and my sister bloggers at Inspy Romance. These folks make a difference in my life every single day. I'm thrilled to walk beside them as we tell stories for Jesus!

Thank you to my Facebook friends, followers, street team, and reader group members for prayers, encouragement, and great fellowship. If you'd like to join other readers who love my stories, please find us at Valerie Comer: Readers Group.

Thanks to my husband, Jim, whose love for me never fails and who encourages me in every endeavor. Thanks to my kids, their spouses, and my wonderful grandgirls for cheering me on. To them, having an author for a mom/grandma is "normal." Imagine that!

All my love and gratitude goes to Jesus, the One who is my vision, the High King of Heaven, the lord of my heart. Thank you. A thousand times, thank you.

THE
COWBOY'S
Reluctant Bride

VALERIE COMER

CHAPTER 1

J ericho!" Sawyer Delgado bellowed his nephew's name as the kid slid off the rail fence amid a frenzy of bawling calves and billows of dust. "Nooo!"

Sawyer pivoted Debonair into the melee, his heart in his throat and his gaze lassoed to the spot where the child-size Stetson had disappeared. The wiry pinto cut between dozens of five-hundred-pound calves. How could this have happened? The five-year-old knew better. Who'd even let the boy near the sorting pens? And where was his father, Sawyer's brother Kade?

Totally oblivious, that's where.

Sawyer broke through the corral dust and pulled Debonair to a halt.

His nephew grinned up at him from a closed-off chute, his eyes bright with excitement. "Uncle Sawyer! Those calves are *crazy!*"

They were. Sawyer willed his heart rate to slow down, but superimposed on the boy was a vision of what could have been: Jericho's body battered by sharp hooves, his skull broken, blood everywhere. He closed his eyes for a brief moment, but that was even worse, since there was no reality to block the nightmare of his buddy's horrific rodeo accident a few weeks back.

Sawyer forced his breathing to steady and stared out at the mountains beyond his father's western Montana ranch, far from that Texas arena. When he could trust his voice, he turned back to his nephew. "You okay, Jer?"

The boy frowned in confusion. "Yeah, why?"

"You scared me when you jumped off the fence." Nothing had ever frightened Sawyer Delgado before that last rodeo. "I thought you'd fallen in with the calves." The calves that were now milling on the other side of the corral, far from Debonair.

"Sawyer!" bellowed Kade. "Get over here and grab this steer!"

Debonair danced in place as Sawyer pinned his nephew with a glare. "Stay outside the sorting pens. All the way outside."

"I'm safe here. See, there's a gate."

"Outside."

Jericho rolled his eyes and clambered over the rails to the grass beyond. He raised his eyebrows as though to ask if his surly uncle was happy now.

Sawyer nodded. "Stay there." Then he turned Debonair back into the corral where Trevor and Kade struggled to hold a rambunctious steer in the vaccination chute.

"Quit your sightseeing and get in here," Trevor

growled, leaning his entire weight against the gate while the calf tried to break free.

Sawyer looped Debonair's reins over a post and jumped in, freeing Trevor to hop over the rails to load the syringe with the four-way solution. Trevor reached through the chute's rails, massaged a flap of skin on the calf's shoulder, and plunged the needle in.

The steer went ballistic, kicking and bawling, but Sawyer kept the pressure tight on the gate at its heels until Kade opened the head-gate and the calf stampeded out to join its buddies.

Kade slammed the head-gate shut and eyed Sawyer. "What were you doing? That calf nearly shoved through the head-gate while you were off gallivanting."

Sawyer skewered his brother with a look. "From here, it looked like Jericho had fallen into the calf pen." If he ever had kids, he'd take much better care of them. Keep them far from danger.

Kade pivoted, shading his eyes against the October sun. "Is he okay?"

"Yeah." Sawyer took a deep breath. "He'd hopped into the exit chute over there to get a closer look."

The older brother shrugged and turned toward his horse. "He knows to stay out of the way." Kade swung onto Bowen. "I'll get the next calf if you watch the head-gate, Trevor."

Trevor filled the syringe and set it on the table outside the chute. "Ready." He scrambled over the rails.

Did no one around here take safety seriously? One mis-step, and Jericho could have been badly injured or even killed. Their mother should keep her grandkids safe in the house on days like today.

Sawyer shoved aside the inconvenient memory of himself as a kid, far more dare-devilish than Jericho likely dreamed of. He'd hopped right in amongst the calves more than once before darting back out, laughing all the way. He was lucky he'd survived.

The mirage of his friend's accident began to sift over this day's reality, but Sawyer superimposed a memory of Anna Winter. Sometimes that helped block the ugliness, until he remembered how she'd stopped taking his calls.

"Quit spacing out!" bellowed Kade. "Get the gate open."

Sawyer blinked, willing the present to win over the past in any form. He surged up the rails then dropped behind the calf and swung the rear gate shut as Trevor slammed the head-gate and Kade slid off Bowen. Somehow he managed to keep his brain in the game, not daring a glance toward his young nephew, not daring another trip down memory lane.

Finally his sister-in-law approached the corral, and the three brothers clambered out and stripped off their gloves. Kade gave Cheri a kiss. "How did the interviews go?"

His wife grimaced. "Not that great. It's hard to find someone who wants to commute all the way up here, and your mom doesn't want someone who insists on virtual work."

They'd been short a cowboy or two this past year, too. Sawyer's dad and brothers had been mighty glad to have him return to the ranch. Only Dad knew the real reason he was back, though. No one else needed to know.

Kade wrapped an arm around Cheri's waist as they led the way toward the ranch house, Jericho's hand clasped in his dad's free one. Sawyer stifled the longing for a family of his own.

Trevor glanced over as he fell into step. "Man, are you okay? You're not the same since you quit the rodeo."

"I'm fine." Liar. "Just got a jolt from Jericho there."

"Nothing used to scare you." Trevor laughed and clouted Sawyer's shoulder.

"I know." He took a deep breath. "Guess I grew up."

Sawyer had taken two steps up the back steps when his phone chimed with an incoming text. He pulled the device out of his pocket and stared at it for a moment, barely aware of the door shutting behind his brothers.

Anna?

As though just thinking about her had conjured her up. But why now, after three months?

He'd tried to convince himself her disappearance didn't matter. That he didn't even care. She was hardly his first, uh... relationship. But he should have known better than to get involved with someone back home. Buckle bunnies chased rodeo cowboys for the fun and the glory. They had no expectations.

Anna wasn't one of them.

He'd been swept away with her flirty responses to his teasing when he'd been in town for Trevor and Denae's June wedding. It had been fun to needle his brothers at first, but he'd really liked her. She was different. They'd connected a few times over the course of a week or two, texted and called for a few weeks after that, then nothing. As far as he could tell, she'd left Saddle Springs in the rearview mirror, without leaving a trace.

Sawyer wasn't accustomed to being ghosted. It was usually him dishing it out. But he couldn't squash the hope that bubbled up at the thought she was back.

Sawyer, we need to talk.

Not a smiley face in sight. Ominous, and completely unrelated to the teasing texts they'd shared in early summer. He'd rather talk than text, but when he tapped her number, it went straight to voicemail. Okay, fine. He'd do it her way.

Hey, beautiful. I've missed you. As evidenced by the column of texts he'd sent her since her last reply in mid-July.

This time, however, she responded immediately. *I hear you're in Saddle Springs. I'm here for two days. When can I meet you at the fairgrounds?*

Would Sawyer be able to keep his head in the game for the afternoon work? He'd have to, with a reward like this one waiting for him.

ANNA WINTER WRAPPED her bulky sweater around her torso and tied the sash against the chilly evening. There was still a bit of sunshine. That didn't keep it from being cold. Her sweater could keep most of the external chill out, but it did little to thaw the ice in her core.

Seeing Sawyer Delgado again wasn't likely to melt her heart as sight of him had done when they first met. The bold cowboy had been the answer to her very selfish prayer. Now that she was actually praying to a God she had a relationship with, she fervently wished He'd dumped a cold shower on her that June day.

He hadn't.

She paced toward the riverbank, her hiking boots crunching through fallen leaves in vibrant colors. Blue flashed as a Steller's jay took wing across the river, squawking indignantly at being disturbed.

A black pickup wearing the Eaglecrest emblem rattled across the nearby bridge.

Anna wrapped her arms tighter around herself and closed her eyes. *God? I could use a boatload of help here. I know it's my mess, but... please help me.* She watched as the truck turned into the fairgrounds parking lot and pulled up beside her car.

Sawyer jumped out of the cab, his gaze already fixed on hers as he slammed the truck door and started toward her.

He was gorgeous.

She allowed herself a moment to appreciate his total masculine look from brown Stetson to scuffed boots with shades of denim in between, split with a brass-buckled belt. But his face... that was what she'd missed most. His square jaw with its rough scruff, the crooked nose, the inset of his intense eyes.

Anna turned away to break the connection. What had she been thinking, meeting him again? It would have been best to do this by email, but she didn't know how to reach him that way. Or text. But the entire message was too long to tap out.

No. She was doing the right thing. She'd confess. Then they'd talk like two mature adults. He'd sign the papers she'd brought, and he'd drive back over that bridge while she went the other way.

They'd never see each other again, and that was for the best.

"Anna?"

She took a step away as she turned, arms still in protective mode. "Hi, Sawyer."

His eyes caressed her. "You look great. I've missed you." But there was hesitation in his dusky voice.

Totally her fault, showing up three months after their last communication. He was right to be a little wary, but that was better than the anger she deserved. The anger that was sure to come.

She raised her chin slightly. "I, um, have something to tell you."

He scanned her quickly before meeting her eyes again. "Oh?"

Suspicious, was he? He had a right to be. "I... I'm pregnant."

Sawyer reeled back a step as though she'd slapped him. "No way," he breathed.

"I'm sorry. I should have known better..." The thing was, she *had* known better. She'd taken a gamble she now regretted.

He shook his head. "It took two."

It definitely had, and those were memories she'd like to erase. "I want to put the baby up for adoption. I shouldn't have taken a chance. Shouldn't have... you know." She clenched her sweater tighter. "I have papers for you to sign. This doesn't need to affect you at all."

Arms crossed over his jean jacket as his stance widened. "No."

"What?" Tears welled in her eyes. Dratted hormones. "Why?" She hated how weak her words came out even as her gaze locked onto his.

"I'm not going to make a snap decision here, Anna. You've had a bit of time to think about this." Those eyebrows rose into his thick hair. "How long, exactly, have you known?"

"Late July," she whispered.

"Before I came home that time and tried, repeatedly, to get in touch with you."

Anna chomped on her lip until she felt the pain of it. "Yes."

"I can count to nine as well as anyone else. You're what, four months along?"

She nodded.

"So there's no rush to make a decision. A few weeks won't matter."

"I can't stay."

"Sure, you can."

"No. I have a job in Bozeman—"

"I'll offer you a job here. What are you making? I'll pay you that, and your medical expenses and free rent besides."

Anna lurched back a step as she stared at him. "What? No." Whatever he was offering, she wasn't taking it.

"Mom's looking for someone to take over some of the office duties at the ranch."

"But then..."

Sawyer leaned in a little, his dark eyes sharp. "Then she'd find out? Yeah, she would. My parents will know, anyway. Because I'll tell them."

"No..." It was hard enough without that. Why did he think she'd quit her job at the Branding Iron and left Saddle Springs?

He grimaced. "It's not like they think I'm an angel, Anna. I've done my best to flaunt my lifestyle in front of my family, but you know what? I'm done with all that. I'm back at Eaglecrest for good, and I'll do the right thing."

Anna shook her head frantically. "This isn't the right thing. Signing those papers is. Tonight."

Sawyer stepped closer and grasped her arms firmly but gently. "Look at me, Anna."

She didn't want to. She wanted to either tear herself loose and flee or throw herself into his strong arms. But she forced herself to meet his gaze. Oh, those eyes.

"You want my cooperation? It comes at a cost."

Everything always did, but this price was too high.

"You come to Eaglecrest. There's an empty apartment, so don't worry about that part. I'm not asking you to move in with me."

Her face heated.

"Give me at least one month. No, until after Christmas. If we can't come to an agreement on a different plan by December thirty-first, I'll sign your papers and you can do whatever you want. I'll pay all the medical expenses for... our baby. No matter what we decide."

She'd still have about six weeks on her own in the new year before giving birth. But he was asking for even more time than that now. Time in which she'd face his family's accusations and see him every day. She couldn't. She just couldn't. Anna tilted her chin up, trying for defiance. "Or what?"

"In Montana, a birth mom can't release a baby for adoption without the father's consent. Don't even try to test me. I'll block you. I promise."

Those dark eyes did not waver. How could he know about adoption laws? Did he have more babies stashed around the state? But a guy who had the nerve to ride wild mustangs had little to fear from a weak woman like her. She'd build a cage for her heart and lock it away. By the time February was over, she'd be on her own, all this behind her. Wiser, by far.

"You leave me little choice."

"I know," he said simply, releasing her, then pulled out his phone and tapped it. "Mom?" But his gaze was riveted on Anna's. "You might want to close down the office assistant ad. I've hired someone for you."

The Cowboy's Reluctant Bride
Montana Ranches Christian Romance 6
coming Spring 2020

ABOUT THE AUTHOR

Valerie Comer lives where food meets faith in her real life, her fiction, and on her blog and website. She and her husband of over 35 years farm, garden, and keep bees on a small farm in Western Canada, where they grow and preserve much of their own food.

Valerie has always been interested in real food from scratch, but her conviction has increased dramatically since God blessed her with four delightful granddaughters. In this world of rampant disease and pollution, she is compelled to do what she can to make these little girls' lives the best she can. She helps supply healthy food — local food, organic food, seasonal food — to grow strong bodies and minds.

Valerie is a *USA Today* bestselling author and a two-time Word Award winner. She is known for writing engaging characters, strong communities, and deep faith laced with humor into her green clean romances.

To find out more, visit her website www.valeriecomer.com where you can read her blog, and explore her many links. You can also find Valerie blogging with other authors of Christian contemporary romance at Inspy Romance.

Why not join her email list where you will find news, giveaways, deals, book recommendations, and more? Your thank-you gift is *Promise of Peppermint*, the prequel novella to the Urban Farm Fresh Romance series.

http://valeriecomer.com/subscribe